Lublin

Lublin

Manya Wilkinson

SHEFFIELD – LONDON – NEW YORK

First published in 2024 by And Other Stories
Sheffield – London – New York
www.andotherstories.org

1 3 5 7 9 8 6 4 2

ISBN: 9781913505943
eBook ISBN: 9781913505950

Editor: Tara Tobler; Copy-editor: Madeleine Rogers; Proofreader:
Sarah Terry; Typesetter: Tetragon, London; Typefaces: Albertan Pro
and Linotype Syntax (interior) and Stellage (cover); Series cover
design: Elisa von Randow, Alles Blau Studio, Brazil, after a concept by
And Other Stories; Author photo: Christopher James Owens.

And Other Stories books are printed and bound in the UK on FSC-
certified paper. The covers are of G . F Smith 270gsm Colorplan card,
which is sustainably manufactured at the James Cropper paper mill
in the Lake District, and are stamped with biodegradable foil.

A catalogue record for this book is available from the British Library.

And Other Stories gratefully acknowledge that our work is
supported using public funding by Arts Council England.

For my grandparents, Bertha and Isidore Greenblatt

I

The sky is as bright as a polished shoe. Elya has never known a sky like it. Over Mezritsh, the sky is often dark with fumes from the tanneries, smoke, ash, cinders, wood shavings, winged insects, small birds, flying cats, prayers, curses and avenging visions of Adoshem. Here on the open road a lad can breathe. Elya fills his lungs. Everything around him is alive and vibrant. With a joyous gasp, he tries to take it all in, pitying the poor unfortunates who have not been invited on this excellent trip, the twins Yossel and Yankel, Benyamin, Szymen, Benesh, Shloymele, Nahum, Moishe Fishben, Moishe Untermeyer, and all the others. How they must envy Elya, Kiva and his cousin Ziv, three trainee merchants headed for the great markets of Lublin to sell brushes. 'Lublin!' Elya cries, and they all cheer. They grab, push and shove each other playfully, Ziv snatching their shoulders, Kiva and Elya running away, Ziv catching and pummelling Kiva. 'Hit him in the *kishkas*,' Elya cries with delight.

The road, which is wide, flat and smooth, becomes even wider, flatter and smoother. Unclenching his fists and throwing back his shoulders, Ziv glides ahead of the others with his seldom-used long-legged stride. When he runs, it's impossible to catch him. Thin and hard, Ziv should have been fast like a tall, slender dog, but he's often droopy and slow, walking as if he's just staggered through a twelve-hour shift at one of the brush and bristle factories in town. But now he walks with a spring in his step.

'Adoshem makes beautiful roads,' observes Kiva. In his well-constructed shoes and superior socks, Kiva walks briskly too, for Kiva. At this rate, they'll reach Lublin in no time. And Elya, who is like an arrow pointed at a target, unexpectedly stops to laugh. I told you, he must be thinking. I promised. But have they got the stamina? This important question prompts him to propose the best way of walking, gently pointing out his friends' mistakes. Ziv, although gaining speed, does not lift his feet high enough and is liable to trip and fall. Kiva lifts his feet too high, coming down on his toes as if stepping over something unpleasant, and will soon tire.

'Watch me,' Elya says.

They watch him with growing irritation.

'We know how to walk, chicken-head.' Ziv reckons he's a better walker than Elya any day. Kiva would rather not walk at all and wishes for a troika with deep upholstered seats.

'Two troikas,' says Elya, 'are speeding down a highway going in opposite directions. One troika is driven by a man, the other by a woman. The woman leans out of her carriage and yells, "Chazzer!"

How dare she?

In response, the angry man leans out of his carriage and yells "Tsoyg!"

They continue on their way, but as the man rounds the next bend he crashes into a chazzer *standing in the middle of the road, killing both himself and the pig.*

If only men would listen.'

'Listen to what?' Ziv doesn't get it. 'Women don't drive troikas.'

Kiva doesn't like it either. *Tsoyg* is a rude word. He asks Adoshem who does miracles to help Elya tell more respectful jokes. Then Ziv needs to stop and pee. Prone to faintness of the kidneys from the beatings he gives and takes in the back alleys of Mezritsh, he pees against a hedge at the side of the road. Kiva, out of sympathy, pees too. Elya has a great joke about peeing, but he won't tell it. Not now. He wants to, but he won't because his *pisher* friends, you should excuse the expression, have no sense of humour. Never mind, they're on their way. Kiva blesses the road and the emptiness of the road, both sides of the road, the middle of the road, the sky above the road, and the birds in the sky above the road, the hedge on which Ziv pees, and the leaves on the hedge on which Ziv pees.

Is he finished?

Not yet.

Kiva blesses their conversation, which immediately dries up. Then he calls down blessings on Elya's vision and Ziv's bladder. Let nothing obstruct either.

Kiva prays at every fork in the road, over every dead animal flattened under the wheels of a troika, before every sip of water, every meal, every snack. Upon seeing anything beautiful, smelling anything nice, wearing anything new, hearing good news, or bad. There's even a prayer in celebration of moving one's bowels after a period of constipation. Praising and offering, thanking and requesting, Kiva talks to Adoshem as if He were another trainee merchant walking alongside them. When Kiva pauses to pray, Elya and Ziv must stand with their hands clasped. When he's finished, they must say 'Amen', pronounced Aw-main, in unison. Later it will be different. Even now they show some impatience. Enough already! They're on the open road, not in a shul. They pass around the flask of water they carry, Kiva reciting a short blessing before they drink. 'That won't improve it,' says Ziv, who does not like the taste of flask water but drinks anyway.

Soon the road narrows to a carriage track meandering through a field and into a forest. Elya eyes the landscape greedily, turning his head this way and that. At the side of the road, in a copse of trees with smooth grey bark and hairy leaves, they forage for walking sticks. 'Over here,' Elya calls out. He cuts sticks for Kiva, Ziv and himself, trimming the leaves.

'Don't we need permission?' Kiva asks, peering nervously through his tight iron spectacles. According to Ziv, wealthy Poles from Warsaw own these woods, or Russians living even further away. 'Nothing to worry about,' he smiles slyly. 'Of course, if we happen to meet a land *Kapitan*, run!' The local *Kapitans* protect the absent landlords' estates, flogging peasants or poor travellers who dare to trespass. 'The peasants should own this land,' Ziv declares. Which is another one of his daft ideas. Peasants owning land? Then he smiles, dazzling them with his big, white teeth. Everyone else has small teeth, bad teeth, no teeth. Only Ziv's teeth, which he won't have for long, are perfect. 'Aren't you going to bless the peasants?' he asks Kiva. 'You blessed everything else.' But Kiva decides to reserve his blessings.

United by tradition and strong faith, the noble peasants, Ziv explains, share tools, labour and the cigarettes they roll from home-cured tobacco. Having little care for privacy, peasants *essen* from a common pot, *shlofen* in a common bed, and *kakken* in the open air, all healthy, normal, and natural. Kiva listens with distaste. He wouldn't like to share a bed or bowl with others, or do his business in the open air. But the forest, shimmering in the sun, is most attractive.

'The Tsar comes here to shoot birds,' Ziv reports.

'Here?'

'Hereabouts. He was shooting birds when *his* workers, as he calls them, aroused by foreigners and *Yiddisher menschen*, marched on the Winter Palace.'

Ziv prepares to talk at length about the revolutionary movement but neither Kiva nor Elya want to hear more. Beyond the forests, there are streams and lakes, grassland, hills and valleys. In every direction there are wonders: a row of bushes with waxy leaves; trees thick with branches; creeping plants and climbing plants; berries ripening in the sun; moss growing in the shady places;

and a deep, consoling silence unimaginable in Mezritsh, where *Yiddisher menschen* shout, cry, joke, argue, or loudly lament the price of eggs, nuts, pelts, and shoes.

Elya thinks back. The day has not started well. Kiva and Ziv were late to the marketplace where they'd arranged to meet Elya. At last they appear. Dressed as if for a Jewish holiday, Kiva Goldfarb is wearing a fine black coat, although it is too warm for such a garment, and walking shoes imported from Berlin. On his head, a new hat. Ziv Nagelbach, with his shabby coat and famished appearance, resembles one of the bristleworkers he admires. 'Hey ear-face!' he greets Elya.

Elya Grynberg turns red. Like *cheder yinglach*, they shove and elbow each other affectionately. Kiva alone has gone on to study Talmud Torah in yeshiva, ten hours a day, six days a week. Kiva has nice clothes, lovely light eyes and round cheeks. His sister Mindel and all the girls on the riverbank adore him. Before he marries, however, he must have nothing to do with women or girls. Nevertheless, he's in demand as a prospective bridegroom and his mother is already taking bids from interested parties. He also has a blue certificate, paid for by his Uncle Velvel, exempting him from military service. What more could a boy want?

Elya runs up to them, anxious for their journey to begin. Along with his personal belongings and a bedroll, Ziv is carrying their sack of provisions, bread, potatoes, and a bucket of soup. Kiva is carrying the brushes they will sell in a large holdall stamped with the company name, VELVEL GOLDFARB & NEPHEW LTD. in gold shadow lettering.

'Careful,' Elya tells him. 'All set?' he asks.

'We were just talking,' Kiva says. 'It's such a long way.'

His cousin Ziv hovers at his elbow.

'What do you mean? Of course it's a long way.' Elya's baffled but

11

there's a bad feeling in the pit of his stomach. Has Kiva changed his mind?

He has.

'Many apologies,' Kiva says, smiling and flinching.

Kiva's not a healthy boy. What if he has a fit on the road? His lungs are delicate. What if he coughs blood? He'll be far from the paper tubes he spits into every morning and the jars of creosote into which these tubes must be thrown.

'But . . . but . . .'

Tears gather in Elya's eyes and he blinks them away. He tells himself to calm down. Calm down and think. Then he remembers the library book on selling, arguing and persuasion he has read. 'I hear what you're saying, Kiva.' He shifts his pack higher. 'We'll start slow. Build up our pace. I've studied the route. We can't get lost.' He takes a deep breath. 'We'll rest. Or catch a troika, stay at an inn. Make it a holiday.'

'No crude carts,' Kiva insists. He will be sick from jostling in a no-frills cart or wagon.

'Of course not,' says Elya. 'But we all need jobs. We can go on the road in the fresh clean air selling brushes, setting our own pace, enjoying the freedom and each other's company, or we can toil in a noisy, dark factory.'

Elya waits, eyebrows up.

'It's good honest labour in those factories,' Ziv protests, though he's never had a job in his life. Roughly he snaps open the holdall and shows Elya one of the paintbrushes they'll be selling. 'Hog bristles,' he sneers.

What did Ziv expect? This is their first time. But even Elya's disappointed.

'My uncle's doing us a big favour,' Kiva reminds them.

'He's cheating us,' says his cousin Ziv, who's from the poor side of the family. 'These are *drek*.'

Ziv corners a man who's pushing a cart filled with onions across the marketplace, and offers him a brush. 'What do you think, eh? *Shlock*, eh? *Drek*? Here, take it.' He gives it to the man for free.

Elya looks on helplessly. 'OK. We won't go,' he says.

Kiva and Ziv nod, shoulder their packs and turn towards home. 'Do you really want to live off your mothers forever?' Elya calls after them. 'All right, I'll go on my own.' He grabs the brush case and the food and begins to stagger away. The brush case alone weighs 0.58 of a pood in the Russian Imperial measurement which is Elya's measurement. 'Why'd you even come this morning? You tricked me,' he snivels. 'I'll tell everyone. The whole town what you did.'

Kiva and Ziv ignore him.

'It isn't real life,' Elya tries again. 'It's on the road. We'll roast food on sticks, stay up all night, laugh when we feel like it, get into mischief and no one'll know.'

'Except the All-Seeing One,' says Kiva, turning around to face him. But from Ziv there's a glimmer of interest. He wants a few words with Kiva and the two confer.

Meanwhile the marketplace is getting busier. Soon Elya's mother will arrive with her eggs to sell. In desperation, Elya opens Kiva's oversized, overpacked backpack and starts throwing the contents on the ground. 'Look at this. Kiva's brought a pillow.' He buries his face in it, smells valerian drops. Ziv laughs. Kiva snatches it away. Underneath the pillow, books. Elya picks one up. It's bound in calfskin with a golden spine. He holds it inches above the cobbles.

'Don't,' Kiva begs. A holy book must never touch the ground. In response Elya lowers the book a bit more. Desecrating books is something Elya's brother Fishel might do. Or Ziv. But Elya's doing it.

'All right. I'll go!' Kiva gasps.

'Ziv?'

Ziv nods, thinking of all the forbidden things he might encounter.

After carefully repacking Kiva's bag, Elya agrees not to walk or carry on the Sabbath.

'Or tie a knot,' Kiva adds. 'No planting or ploughing, cooking or boiling, hunting or trapping, lighting or extinguishing fires, scraping or sanding.'

Elya promises. They divide the packs between them, vow never to argue again, and set off down the road, shoulder to shoulder.

Elya Grynberg, fourteen years old, has finally left home. In the large suitcase they will carry in turn, Kiva's uncle has packed twenty-four boxes of paintbrushes, twenty brushes to a box, 480 brushes in all, encased for protection in moss litter, also used for the lining of mittens and boots because it absorbs twenty times its weight in water. Unworldly Kiva, who loves Adoshem, soft benches, prune pastries and his father's gold watch, which will be stolen on the journey; who hates discomfort, dark forests, insects, Cossacks, swearing, sleeping outside and walking, is first to *shlep* the brush case. Ziv, who loves all workers but hates work, will take the brush case next although not for long because, *oy vey*, his arm hurts. Then it's Elya's turn. Elya, who loves jokes, maps, commerce, money; who hates his big ears, his father's shoemaking, his mother's chickens and admitting he's wrong, will hold the brush case tenderly, solemnly and without complaint.

'*Three boys and their guide are journeying through Poland on their way to sell brushes in Lublin,*' says Elya. '*They walk and walk, but never arrive. Are they walking in circles?*

"*We're lost,*" *cries one of the boys.* "*And I thought you were the best guide in Poland.*"

"*I am,*" *says the guide.* "*But we've wandered into Moldavia.*"'

Stony faces all around. Even Elya's not pleased. There's something wrong with the punchline.

'*We've wandered into Ruthenia,*' he tries again.
Still not right.
Hungary? Lithuania? Bohemia? Silesia? Galicia?
Never mind. They're on their way.

II

There's a mill in Mezritsh belonging to Kiva's father; a brickyard; a cigarette factory; a rope-twisting factory; an eau de cologne factory; a soap factory; shuls, naturally, where fathers pray for the success of their sons; a tannery; and many brush and bristle factories known far and wide. Mezritsh, as Elya would tell you, is the brush and bristle capital of the world. The very air, when the wind comes from the right direction, smells like hair. Not just any hair. Pig hair, constricting the lungs.

The surrounding land belongs to the Polish Count Potocki. The family coat of arms, a yellow cross with three branches, one broken, is rumoured to signify shameful apostasy. Years ago, a Potocki was cut off when he became, you should excuse the expression, a Jew, and took the name Abraham, which is hard to believe. A Russian church is the tallest building in town. But don't look up. The shadow of its spire and cross might fall on you. And then what? Dropsy, blindness, bad knees.

The road from Mezritsh to Lublin climbs along the crest of a hill, woodland on both sides. It's too narrow to walk three abreast and Ziv tries to take the lead, cutting ahead of Elya. Then Elya cuts ahead of Ziv.

But where's Kiva?

Bringing up the rear.

Kiva is cautious. Maybe too cautious. But you need a cautious friend on a trip like this. Kiva will never let them get into trouble, or take unnecessary risks. He's always on the alert for Cossacks who may suddenly appear carrying sabres, long spears, horseman's picks, axes and pistols. Kiva's come on this trip to satisfy his mother, who desires him to enter his rich Uncle Velvel's business against her husband's wishes. Kiva's father, an ill-tempered miller by day and a passionate scholar by night, wants his son to study Torah around the clock. Kiva wants to please both his father and his mother. But how? Now his mother is pleased but his father isn't.

Swatting at small bushes, wildflowers and the trunks of young trees with his walking stick, Ziv would rather displease. But you need a naysayer on a trip like this to question the wisdom of the leader. And who's the leader?

Elya, naturally.

They gallop down the road to Lublin, imagining they're horses, passing no one except a long line of students, some no older than children. Where are they going? The yeshiva in Biale, a town famous for its piety. For the briefest moment, Kiva has the urge to join them. 'Come with us,' they call out to him. But Kiva's on a different path. All the students, even the youngest, have beards. Beards that are tufts, tassels, bookmarks, handkerchiefs; beards resembling shreds of tobacco, lady's slippers, and the crests of birds; flat-bottomed beards and pointy beards; tall and fragrant beards; beards with length and breadth but no thickness; beards like clouds, like hedges; beards like Adoshem's.

Even the girls?

No. Girls are not students.

To his shame, Ziv is still beardless. It's unmanly. He should be wearing Kiva's beard, which is fair in colour. Or Elya's, which is coming in short, black and bristly. 'Sorry,' Kiva says to Ziv. 'If I could, I'd share mine with you.' That's Kiva, generous to a fault. But Ziv sulks. 'I didn't like my beard at first, then it grew on me,' says Elya. But Ziv's not amused. Another *pish*? Why not? Ziv asks his friends to stop while he pees into a ditch.

The trees along the roadside are taller and fuller now, some with barks of orange and red. Elya stares with delight at row upon row, so tall and straight. All Elya knows are *shtetl* trees: hard trees dropping edible nuts in prickly husks; trembling trees with leaves that flutter in the slightest breeze; trees with leaves resembling feathers that smell bad when touched, with sour berries which could be cooked and eaten and small white flowers which could be turned into syrup and drunk. As for bushes and grasses, Elya knows only common burdock bushes with prickly leaves; bird cherry bushes that line the roads around Mezritsh; and the tall stiff grasses, reeds and rushes that grow along the banks of the Kzrna River.

'What are these trees called?' Elya asks the others, but they don't know. All Kiva knows about trees is the Parable of the Trees, which he believes might have actually occurred.

'When?' Elya taunts, but kindly.

'On the day Abimelech was crowned King of Shechem.'

'Who?' Ziv and Elya nudge each other and laugh.

'Abimelech, the illegitimate son of King Gideon and his concubine.'

'Where's Shechem?' enquires Elya. He couldn't care less.

'In Palestine, between the mountains, Ebal and Gerizim.'

Kiva's knowledge of the Holy Land is prodigious. If only he'd known as much about Poland, things might have turned out differently. Ziv would rather hear about the concubine. According to Kiva, Gideon already has seventy legal wives. Why does he need a concubine? She must be something special.

Then Abimelech grabs the throne, killing all Gideon's other sons and rightful heirs except the youngest who escapes and curses the *narisher menschen* who have accepted a usurper as their king.

'At the same time the trees also seek a king,' Kiva tells them, which Elya rightly regards as ridiculous. He determines to listen no more.

'The olive tree with its silvery leaves is asked if it wants to be King of the Trees.'

'Who asked it? Another tree?' Ziv scoffs.

Is this what Kiva studies all day in yeshiva?

'But the olive tree declines,' says Kiva. 'Why give up its oil to be King of the Trees?'

A tree, Ziv reckons, would be a better ruler than the Tsar. He nudges Elya who nudges him back. Kiva ignores them both. They're missing the point. 'Then they ask the fig tree,' Kiva says. 'But the fig also declines. Why give up its fruits to be King of the Trees? So, they ask the vine, but the vine won't give up its wine.'

As a last resort, they ask the thorn bush, the lowest grade of plant life, according to Kiva.

'I don't understand,' Ziv complains.

'There's nothing to understand, it's just a story,' says Elya.

'It's more than a story. It's a parable,' says Kiva. 'The parable of who should be king.'

According to Kiva, the story compares Abimelech, the usurper, to a thorn bush with its deep and twisting roots grabbing nourishment from the soil, harming other plants and causing headaches for those who cultivate the land. A thorn bush offers no protection to anyone except unclean insects hiding under its brambles. The olive, fig, and vine, however, all know their nature and their place. Unlike Abimelech, they do not covet a position that is not rightfully theirs. 'The present Tsar might be unworthy,' Kiva adds. 'But he's the rightful heir.'

'Says who?' Ziv sneers and wanders off to pee on a cluster of wildflowers.

'Don't you want to know how Abimelech died?' Kiva calls after him. But Ziv doesn't give a *drek*. 'Struck on the head,' says Kiva, 'with a millstone thrown from a tower by a woman. Then, almost dead, he begs his armour-bearer to kill him so that it should not be said that the mighty Abimelech perished at the hand of a *balabusta*.'

Elya thinks immediately of Kiva's mother, the miller's wife. A seat-grabber on carriages and trains. With her big arms, she could lift a millstone.

The sun is now high in the sky and Kiva takes out his father's watch. His mother begged him to leave such a valuable item at home, but where would they be without it? Only 12:05. Excellent time. But as the day advances, the road grows longer and Kiva wonders when they'll be catching a carriage. He would like to stop and rest. But Elya urges him on. 'Soon you'll be resting on a feather-filled Lublin love seat,' says Elya. 'Or on any of the vast and comfortable armchairs in the town.'

Lublin is only 102 kilometres south of Mezritsh. At an average walking pace of six kilometres an hour, walking for eight hours every day, Elya determines that they will arrive in two, maybe three days. In Lublin there are great Jewish marketplaces, Jewish squares; fountains; theatres; stone-built synagogues; renowned yeshivas; statues of *Polisheh* heroes, who are admittedly not Jewish; and statues of frowning lions, who look Jewish with their expressions of finicky distaste as if offered a pork ball or a crustacean to eat. Gazing past distant fields of a lilac hue, Elya imagines Lublin, just there over the horizon waiting to be discovered. Lublin, where all the fortunate inhabitants carry full purses; where Ziv can buy a beard, and Kiva a prune pastry; where the salt is saltier, the water wetter, the streets more than six cobbles wide. It's only a matter of time before Elya and his friends arrive.

Then Ziv needs to stop and *nemen* a piss again.

Late in the afternoon, they find a clearing a short distance from the road and make camp. There's a tranquil lake nearby, clear and deep. The surface, mirror-like, reflects the sky. Parting the reeds that surround the shore, Kiva peers over the still water. 'Maybe we'll find a baby in a basket,' he says. The others look at him like he's crazy. Do they not even know about Moses in the bulrushes? Kiva feels sorry for all those who have not tasted Jewish learning. Standing beside him, Elya admires the flowers with large, round leaves floating on the lake. Elya knows many words but he doesn't know the word for the water plants he sees or the glowing trees that line the opposite shore. All he can do is point and gaze with large foolish eyes.

'Very nice,' says Kiva.

'But do you know their names?'

'Adoshem knows.'

'So you don't know?'

'He named everything.'

'I'm asking you.'

'Ask Adoshem.'

Kiva only knows the names of those trees that appear in the Jewish Bible: olive trees, fig trees, palm trees, caper bush trees and sorb trees, which do not grow in Poland. Passing between two palm trees invites demons, according to Kiva.

But what use has Elya for this nonsense when before him are the real wonders of nature? Even the small insects dancing in the air delight him. 'We could live here,' he says out loud.

What's wrong with him? They can't live here. Here is nowhere. What if Kiva's Uncle Velvel, the Great Benefactor, saw them dawdling beside a common lake, not even a lake, a lakelet? The Uncle, an eagle of understanding, wouldn't understand. Besides which, Elya's not interested in nature. None of them are. They are town *menschen*, not peasants. Even so, Elya wants to stand for a moment and appreciate the view. He wants to, but he won't. Instead, he and Kiva gather dead wood to build a fire. They carry a load between them in Elya's blanket which he loosens from his bedroll. Ziv could carry more wood single-handedly, without a blanket, but looking both tired and sly, he leans against a tree and watches them work.

Kiva cannot start an outdoor fire, although he's willing to learn. Elya claps him on the back and shows him how it's done. First Elya must search for the right spot, away from bushes and overhanging trees. In preparation for this very task, he has read a book on outdoor living and with confidence sends Kiva off to gather tinder.

'*Vas iz* tinder?'

It's the small stuff that ignites easily. Dry grass, of which there's plenty around the campsite; bark and mosses in the surrounding woods. Kiva, who's frightened of woods, hesitates. 'And we need kindling,' Elya calls after him. 'Bigger pieces, twigs, dry leaves.'

Elya, who's decided on a square construction for their first fire, places two large branches side by side, close but not touching, to form a base, then two branches on top. When they break up the larger branches with Elya's axe, Kiva manages only a few unhappy swipes. Never mind, Elya will teach him. What can Kiva teach Elya in return? How to admire Adoshem? Elya doesn't want to learn that. But Kiva, wiping his hands on his fine trousers, decides to teach him anyway. Then kneeling, Kiva starts to blow, while Elya lights the tinder with a match. Such a long time it takes, Kiva is soon dizzy and out of puff.

Meanwhile, somewhere in England, a man with the English name of Robert Baden-Powell is setting forth the principles of Boy Scouting. Gathering twenty-one lads from all backgrounds, *arumloifers* included, he sends them on a week-long outdoor camp in the English countryside to test his methods, encouraging the boys to organise themselves in packs and select a leader like Elya.

Once the fire is going, Elya spreads the tarpaulin he's brought. Then he and Kiva lay out soup, cheese, hard-boiled eggs, fresh bread. A feast!

'Isn't this great?'

From under his tree, Ziv nods lightly. He will allow it's been a good day and a good meal is coming.

Then Kiva lifts his head. 'Did you hear that?' he asks, his chubby cheeks turning pale.

'What?'

'I heard it,' says Ziv, getting to his feet.

Like a whistle in the air, the sound comes first from the left, then the right, from above, then below. 'We're surrounded!' Kiva cries, his cheeks now white as two boiled potatoes. 'Cossacks!' he screeches, as small whistling birds rise up out of the grass all around them and fly away.

When two Christian children are found dead in the town of Kishinev, an angry mob led by Cossacks start a pogrom, believing Jews used the children's blood to prepare the matzohs eaten on Passover. What, matzohs? That's ridiculous. Matzohs are made only from wheat which is never exposed to moisture or allowed to ferment in any way.

In Kishinev, the local police make no attempt to stop the mob. Nails are driven through Jewish heads, bellies split and filled with feathers. Many decide this is the last straw and make plans to leave for America where there are no angry mobs, no graveyard ghosts, starving birds with sooty wings, muddy puddles, damp walls, or bleak faces. Whole families depart. Even girls. Girls, it is said, who were ugly in Mezritsh become beautiful in America. Why stay?

What are they called, those little birds, Elya wonders, bending over the good fire he's built, while Ziv gets out his slingshot and takes aim.

'Put that away!' Elya cries.

A moment later he gets up and shakes himself, as if waking from a dream. Elya doesn't care about birds. All he cares about is commerce. Yet he finds himself trying, over and over again, to imitate their whistling song, giving Ziv a headache. Kiva only knows those birds unfit to eat: birds that inhabit the ruins of Babylon, and birds that dwell in the clefts of desert rocks.

The Audubon Society for the protection, preservation and appreciation of birds has recently been established beyond the borders of Poland. The Society's main purpose is to convince women like Elya's mother to cease buying, wearing or admiring feathered hats. No feathered hats? A bird in Poland only exists for its hat feathers.

Nursing a sore head, Ziv watches while his friends recommence unpacking. Using Elya's pocket knife, which he sharpens on his shoe, Ziv whittles the end of his walking stick to a point.

'Too bad about his head,' observes Elya.

'It's not his head,' Kiva whispers.

'His neck?'

'No, not his neck.'

'His arm?'

'No, not that either.'

'Then what?'

But Kiva won't say.

Elya has made a cooking crane with his shovel, leaning it at just the right angle against a heavy log placed on one side of the fire, then hanging their soup pot from the handle.

When the soup starts bubbling, Elya calls them to eat.

But where's Kiva?

Praying.

The setting sun grows enormous, then sinks below the horizon. Kiva makes two more blessings. One for the setting sun, another for the food they are about to share.

'Like peasants,' Ziv says.

Frowning, Kiva shakes out a linen napkin. Where did he get that? Ziv throws a hard-boiled egg at him. 'Catch, chubby cheeks.'

The egg hits Kiva in the chest and falls to the ground.

'Hey,' Elya cries. 'We might need that.'

'Sorry,' says Kiva. But it's Ziv who should be sorry.

Kiva has a clever collapsing cup which he folds and unfolds like a magician, then allows Ziv to do it. 'Thanks.' Ziv catches him in a tender headlock, then lets him go.

An indoor boy who drinks raisin wine on the Sabbath, Kiva honours his father with a silver medal won for Torah study, and carries numerous pairs of shoes along with a supreme, stainless pillow in his oversized backpack. Waving his linen napkin, he blesses even the dirt already beginning to accumulate under his fingernails.

After eating and drinking, they dig a latrine near the edge of the woods. Elya digs then gives the shovel to Kiva. Kiva recites a blessing, loads the shovel with earth, but can't lift it. 'Sorry.' He tries again, taking less this time. His father, the miller, can heft a five-pood sack of flour, sometimes two at once. 'I'll toughen you up,' Elya promises. 'Watch me.' He feels great affection for Kiva, whose chubby cheeks are now red as plums.

Ziv can't dig. The pain in his head has travelled to his shoulder. If Ziv could dig, he'd dig a better, deeper latrine than Elya or Kiva.

'Too bad about his shoulder,' observes Elya.

'It's not his shoulder,' Kiva whispers.

'His back?'

'Not his back.'

'His feet? Knees? Elbows? Legs?'

'It's his haemorrhoids.'

'*Vas iz* haemorrhoids?' Elya asks.

'*Tsores.*'

Something painful upon which Ziv is forced to perch, haemorrhoids are like a ball of mud stuck through with twigs, brambles and burrs clinging to the seat of his pants.

After dinner, they roast potatoes. 'Go on, Kiva.' Ziv hands him a potato on a stick. The skin is charred black and covered in ash. Kiva looks at it dubiously. 'That's the best part,' Ziv tells him.

It's still too hot, and Kiva burns his mouth eating it off the stick. '*Wasser*!' he cries, and Ziv splashes him with water from their flask. 'Sorry,' Kiva says once more, as if it were his fault. And perhaps it is. Before taking a bite he has forgotten the blessing. *Wasser* drips from his face to his chest, soaking his shirt. Then Ziv jumps on him and motions Elya to join in. They wrestle Kiva to the ground and give him dead limbs. Kiva tries to get up. He can't feel his arms or legs. Well that's the whole point. Now he's hopping on one leg, one arm dangling. They howl with laughter, Kiva howling loudest.

III

As the night deepens and darkens, they talk about girls. Kiva, while professing no interest, is the real expert on females. He has an older sister, Mindel, to whom he is particularly close. Elya remembers them play-fighting on the riverbank in Mezritsh. Big Mindel pinning Kiva down. Kiva squealing, kicking his feet, scrabbling at her long skirt and pawing her thighs.

Elya never mentions his sisters, Rifka and Zusa. What's there to say? Poor Rifka is already taller than all the other girls her age, and who'll want to marry a tall girl? Baby Zusa, nearly four, is not such a baby any more but still attached to Rifka by a length of clothesline. Consequently, Elya knows nothing about women and girls. But Kiva has learned a lot from Mindel and he's ready to share. Night rags and blood, for example, are things Kiva knows that neither Ziv nor Elya has ever heard about. Night rags? Blood? What does this have to do with women and girls? But Kiva has already said too much and will say no more. 'I can't,' he tells them. 'Sorry.' But they hold him down. Tickle and rabbit punch him until he relents. Ziv's punches, hard, sharp and sneaky, are particularly persuasive. The truth is even more disturbing than they expect and Elya accuses Kiva of lying.

'Once a month?'

'He's joking.'

'I'm not.'

'Says who?'

'Mindel told me.'

'Down there?'

'She's having you on.'

'You'll see Elya. You too Ziv.'

Ziv is practically betrothed to one of the riverside girls called Shayna. But plain-faced Shayna would rather have Elya. Unfortunately Elya is already betrothed to Libka and had Libka's father not been such a careless smoker, Elya and Libka would have married one day.

Kiva thinks Libka's too skinny. He is not impressed with Shayna either who's not as skinny as Libka but nevertheless not a *gezunteh moid* like Mindel.

Ziv thinks Mindel is fat and Shayna is ugly. Face? Feh. Hair? Frizzy. Chest? Flat. If you separate all the girls on the riverbank into *mieskiets* and doves, Shayna would definitely be a *mieskiet*. Ziv would rather have Libka any day, and is considering ways to steal her from Elya, who doesn't appreciate her or so Ziv thinks.

How does it feel to want to steal another lad's fiancée? Good. It feels good if you're Ziv. What if Elya were to meet with an accident on the road? Tumbled from a tree? Buried in a gravel pit? Brained with a walking stick? Or drowned in a common lake? Surely Ziv's better-looking. He peers into the small mirror he's hidden in his pocket and practises his famous scowl. What a couple they'd make.

The most beautiful girl in Mezritsh, Libka Rabinowitz should have been crowned 'Miss Mezritsher Marketplace, Purim Queen, 1906', but the title went to a snooty rich girl, *Herr Doktor*'s daughter, Channa, rumoured to have a bath every day; her own bed in her own bedroom; a kerosene night light, thin as a finger; and a bear cub lying on her pillow. Channa cannot imagine playing in a courtyard; eating black bread smeared with chicken fat; kissing a herring; sleeping in a cold room without a night light; hiding in a barrel; falling into a ditch; or boarding a crowded train.

'Wipe out the rich,' Ziv hollers, grabbing his cousin Kiva by the neck. Kiva falls helplessly to the ground. Closing his eyes, he makes a prayer face, steadying himself for the next humorous assault.

'At the funeral of a rich man,' Elya says, 'a stranger joins the mourners and begins weeping and wailing.

"Are you a relative?" someone asks.

"No," the stranger says.

"Then why are you crying?"

"That's why."'

Blank faces all around.

'Is it funny?' Elya asks, taut-shouldered.

It's so unfunny, Ziv challenges Elya to a duel with walking *shteks*, cutting and thrusting to unlock Elya's defences, then employing the 'flunge', a flying lunge giving himself the element of speed and surprise; then the lesser-known 'beat', a *zetz* similar to one used in boxing. Afterwards, Ziv sets a spare potato on fire for fun. 'What we need now is rye beer.' Amicably he knuckles the side of Kiva's head. 'Get off,' Kiva shouts, glasses askew. Soon they're all throwing clods of earth at each other, ducking and laughing. Ziv, who is still hungry, who was born hungry, takes another potato. Perhaps he has worms in his *kishkas*. Cheeks bulging, he stuffs the whole thing in at once, fearful someone will take it off him. Kiva, despite burning his mouth, would also like another, but doesn't want to eat more than his fair share. Ziv eats his fair share and Kiva's.

'Have you heard what women are doing?' Ziv asks, mouth full. 'Last winter, they marched in London to demand their rights. It was raining and those *meshugeneh* women marched back and forth in the mud. Can you imagine it?' Ziv sticks out an elbow, jabs Kiva and winks.

Frankly, they can't. They know about processions and parades, but women's marches? Only armies march.

'*Vas iz* rights?' asks Kiva.

'They want to vote. Those English women.'

'*Oy,*' says Kiva, 'don't let this reach my Uncle Velvel's ears.'

London, England is a dim, faraway place. The only thing they recognise in this *farkakta* story is mud, which may be encountered in Poland any time of year, frozen, wet, or dried to dust.

Ziv calls himself enlightened. He reads Russian novels from the town library. That's Ziv, capacious of mind. And Kiva? Kiva has a loquacious big sister. There's only Kiva and Mindel in Kiva's family. There were others, of course, lost in the last diphtheria epidemic and Kiva still remembers his dead *shvesters aun bruders,* their swollen cheeks and blueish skin. *Herr Doktor* tries opening a vein under their tongues and letting blood to no avail. An anti-toxin serum made from horses might have saved them, but it's not available in the Pale of Settlement yet.

Kiva will be the only one left when his last surviving sister, Mindel, emigrates to America, which she will soon do. Occasionally she'll send money. Once she'll send a photograph of herself outside a Rexall drugstore in Hoboken, New Jersey, wearing a tippet. Then she'll never be heard of again.

Ziv has many big sisters who ignore him and whom he ignores. His mother is always out working. His father disappeared long ago. Both Kiva and Ziv are precious *ben yochids*, only sons. But Elya is the oldest of five children, if you count his brother Alter who died in infancy. 'It happened so fast, he didn't even know he was dead,' Elya's mother Klara says to her surviving children.

(He knew.)

Elya has nothing to say and thinks he'd better just tell another joke.

When will he learn?

'*Why did the chicken go to the seance?*' he asks.

'I don't know,' Ziv winks, expecting something rude.

'To get to the other side!'

'Huh?' Ziv's let down again. Doesn't Elya know any *shtupping* jokes? Any *putz* jokes?

Elya only knows one.

'An alter moid, *who needs but cannot find a husband, agrees to meet the most undesirable man in Mezritsh and a date is arranged. The night of the date, there's a knock on the door. When she opens the door, the old spinster sees a man with no arms or legs sitting in an invalid's chair on wheels.*

"How can I marry you?" she asks, "you have no legs."

"Which means I can't run out on you."

"You have no arms."

"I can't beat you."

"But are you still good in bed?" she enquires at last.

"I knocked on the door, didn't I?"'

It takes Ziv a minute, then he gets it and he laughs.

Elya has made Ziv laugh!

Ziv nearly pisses himself.

'We need to make an early start tomorrow,' Elya then says.

'Why's that?' Ziv isn't hungry but takes another potato for amusement. 'I thought we might stay up all night. Sleep late tomorrow.'

'We don't want to fall behind, do we?'

'Is that a rule?' Ziv takes one bite of his potato and throws the rest into the long grass.

'No, but the sooner we get to Lublin, the better. Spend less time and money on the road. Sell more in the city. Get a jump on the competition.' Elya gets out his map and shows it to his friends, indicating tomorrow's route. Along a snaking line, various Jewish and peasant villages have been marked and named by the worthy Mezritsher brush merchant who drew the map for Elya, while his fellow *farkoyfers* watched.

'Why don't we have a proper map?' asks Ziv.

'This is a proper map. Look here.'

Elya points to the Village of Lakes; the Village of No Lakes; Russian Town, a dangerous place for Jews; Prune Town, the home of the flakiest crescent pastry; Prayer Town, where men and women walk on separate sides of the street; the Village of Girls, full of beautiful and available young women; the Village of the Dead, so called because no one has ever sold anything there; and the Village of Fools, where a merchant can sell anything.

'Or maybe there are no such places,' Ziv makes a frowning face.

'What do you mean?'

'They just don't sound real.'

'They're real, don't worry.'

'Lemme see that,' Ziv grabs Elya's map. 'A map for children,' he hoots.

Elya grabs it back. He loves maps. Best memory: his father asking to see his atlas.

'Which map?' Elya opens the big book.

'China,' his father, Usher, says.

Does China really exist?

It does.

His sister Rifka wants to see too, but she's discouraged. Maps are not for girls. She's handed her needlework which makes her cry.

'Where shall we stop?' Elya now enquires.

'Prune Town or Prayer Town,' says Kiva. 'Anywhere but Russian Town.'

'As long as I'm navigating,' says Elya, 'we'll avoid it.'

'I'm not,' says Ziv.

'Not what?'

'Avoiding it. Why should we? I won't be kept out by Russians,' he sneers. 'If it's on the way.'

'It's not on the way.'

Elya's mother, Klara, warned him about Russians before he set out.

'If they stop you, you don't know anything, didn't hear anything, didn't see anything, can't remember anything.'

'Anything about what?'

'Anything about anything.' Klara's hand closes around Elya's wrist. 'Call him "The Little Father".'

'Who?'

'The Tsar.'

'He's not my father.'

'Listen to me, Elya, if the Russians hear you praise their Tsar, they'll be merciful. Say he has golden blood.'

'I'm not saying that.'

Elya looks at her and shakes his head. *'The Tsar,'* he jokes, *'disturbed by bad dreams, calls a* farmegn *to the Alexandra Palace to forecast his future. "You'll die on a Jewish holiday," the soothsayer predicts.*

"Which one?" the Tsar asks.

"Any day you die will be a Jewish holiday."'

Klara makes a face. She's got pans to scour. Rummaging through the cutlery, she can't find the spoons. She overcooks the buckwheat, spills the milk and disturbs the sleeping cat. 'Where's Rifka?' she asks the air. Rifka's eating sugar from the sugar bag. 'Rifka,' Klara cries, 'the dentist with his pliers is coming.'

Ziv wants to stop in Girl Town. He puts a match in his mouth and rolls it around between his lips as he's seen the toughest bristleworkers do.

'Hey,' Elya cries, 'we might need that.'

'Gai kakken afen yam,' cries Ziv.

And Kiva turns pale.

'Please,' Kiva begs. 'No more unclean talk.'

'What did I say?'

'I won't repeat it.'

'*Gai kakken*? Was that it?'

'You know it was.'

'I just want to be sure,' Ziv smirks. 'So I don't say it again.'

A natural prankster, Ziv once drank a glass of vodka and swallowed a sardine whole. Now he lets off wind in Kiva's face, and, crying with laughter, Kiva runs away.

'Here's the plan,' says Elya when Ziv stops chasing and Kiva stops running. 'Get up early. Walk all day. No spending money unless absolutely necessary.'

'I thought we were going to have fun,' Ziv mutters.

'Fun?'

'Yeah, fun.'

'But this is business.'

'What do you say Kiva?'

'It's not up to Kiva,' says Elya.

'Who's it up to? You?'

Yes, Elya thinks. He's the leader. He has the vision. All they have to do is follow him. They can have fun any time. Fun doesn't take any effort.

'You can plan all you want, but Adoshem might have other ideas,' says Kiva at last.

'See,' says Ziv.

'This isn't a holiday,' says Elya.

Then Kiva, having unfolded his four-cornered *tallis* with tender care, turns away and begins bobbing in prayer.

'Can you make a girl prayer?' Ziv asks, mischievously creeping up behind him and reaching around to pull his beard.

'What about a money prayer?' asks Elya.

Kiva waves him away.

'So all you have is a prayer prayer?' Ziv scoffs. 'What good is that?' He nudges Elya and they both laugh, still friends after all.

Whooping, they grab Kiva's prayer shawl from off his shoulders and play tug of war with it.

When they undress, Elya is surprised to see Ziv's ropey arms and legs, his ragged underwear, his long penis. In the dim light, Ziv's bruises are not visible. There's no trace of the punches, hooks and jabs that have weakened his kidneys, or the knotty little half-healed wounds on his forearms and legs. Meanwhile Kiva tries to use the latrine but is unsuccessful. As soon as he pulls down his trousers he feels nervous and exposed. The night air on his bottom is inhibiting. He thinks he hears the sound of laughter behind him. Kiva's not afraid to pee, only to do the other thing. He doesn't want his friends to smell his business.

Back at the campsite, undressing modestly under his blankets, Kiva puts on his striped pyjamas and his night shoes. He lays the walking *shtek* he's kept with him all day tenderly beside his bedroll. He is thinking of bringing it back for Mindel.

Can they sleep now?

Not yet.

If Elya will rake some ashes from their campfire and sprinkle them around their bedrolls, Kiva promises they'll see proof of demons in the morning. What proof? Three-toed footprints like that of a large fowl, Kiva guarantees. And poor tired Elya must oblige.

Then they can all go to sleep.

'*Shlof gezunterheit*,' Elya tells them. Only Elya doesn't *shlof*. The earth beneath his bedroll is hard and he's uncomfortable. He gets up and examines the ground. Just as he thought, small rocks and knife-grass, so called because stiff and thorny. He removes the rocks and weeds and he lies down again. Thinking over the occurrences of the day, he cannot settle like the others. Are they so unmoved by the sights and sounds of the road that they can simply sink into oblivion?

35

Ziv's breathing is heavier and slower now. Then he begins to snore. The sound, Elya tries to convince himself, is not so unpleasant. Kiva, on the other hand, hardly makes a noise, fitting snugly into his bedroll, like a foot inside a shoe. His special blankets, produced for herders, prospectors, and explorers, are made of waterproof canvas above and fine wool below, equipped with snaps and rings.

Kiva, however, is only pretending to sleep. Already missing Mezritsh, he cries soundlessly into his pillow so the others won't hear. 'Mindel,' he whispers like a prayer. Just then he feels a chill at his back as if someone, without warning, has opened a window behind him. This sensation is followed by a small but urgent tickle in his throat and he coughs once, twice.

IV

Lying on his side in his bedroll with his legs drawn up, Elya's thinking of his betrothed. There is only the smallest of dowries. Libka's father, cursed with five daughters, can barely make ends meet and her house is even worse than his own. Everywhere there are barrels. These are filled with the ropes with which the family stuff mattresses for a living. The air smells of unmade beds and cigarette smoke. Instead of a proper cooking stove constructed of bricks, there's a tripod balanced over a few pieces of wood.

The first and only time Elya and his mother visit, Elya's uncomfortable. There are not enough chairs and Libka's four little sisters all stand gawping at him. Her bachelor uncle, who lives with them, a heavy man with large features, is shabbily dressed because not all uncles are rich uncles. He crosses his legs, briefly displaying the worn soles of his worn boots. Libka's father's boots are also worn, Elya cannot help but notice. That's enough, he tells himself. He urges himself not to notice shoes or boots again. He may be the son of a shoemaker, but he is not now, and never will be, interested in shoes. He thinks he's in charge of his thoughts, but sometimes his thoughts disobey him.

Libka's father smokes urgently. As soon as he extinguishes one cigarette, he lights another. He even offers one to Klara, who's outraged. Women do not smoke in mixed company, or anywhere outside the privacy of their own homes. In New York City, America, which is never far from Elya's thoughts, *eyn froy* is arrested that very summer for consuming a cigarette in a motor car on Fifth Avenue.

Elya tries to look at Libka without looking like he's looking. All five sisters, fair-haired and slender, hardly there like wisps of smoke with small and delicate pink ears, resemble angels. Or are they just ordinary girls made wraithlike by a poor diet? Dressed in the thinnest of shifts, one sister sticks out her tiny elbow and jabs another. To earn extra for the family, they are sent out into the street every day to collect horse dung for use in the tanneries.

Then Klara's offered a glass of home-brewed schnapps, which is both cloudy and pulpy.

'L'Chayim' and 'L'Shalom'.

After drinking, Libka's bachelor uncle pats the heat from his face. He smiles at Elya the way you smile at someone you don't like. When the rabbi arrives, the marriage contract, written in both Hebrew and Aramaic, is signed. Libka prints her name with much effort. She's only twelve. Then the rabbi dips the nuptial quill in the nuptial ink and hands it to Elya. He signs with a flourish, Klara watching over his shoulder.

A crude version of the ballpoint pen, used only to mark rough surfaces such as animal hides, is currently available in Mezritsh. But the smooth-writing ballpoint, invented in 1938 by László Biró, will not arrive in Poland until 1942, which will be too late for most Mezritshers.

At the conclusion of the signing, a plate is typically broken. But, bad luck, there are no plates to spare. 'Can we set a date?' Elya hears his mother say. 'The sooner the better. Perhaps two weeks,' she suggests.

'Two weeks!' Libka's mother looks up in alarm.

'A summer wedding.'

'So soon?'

'Why not?'

But there's a dress to be made, food to prepare, and musicians to hire. These things will take time and money. Libka's father rests his cigarette on the edge of a barrel and paces.

'Many other girls are interested,' says Klara. Which is not the truth. She takes out her purse. 'You'll pay me back,' she says, 'when you're able.'

It's only then that Elya understands what his mother's up to. She doesn't want him to go on the road to sell brushes in Lublin and has tried everything she can think of to keep him in Mezritsh. He bows his head so that she cannot see the expression on his face.

What's the difference between a dog with big teeth and a Jewish mother?

Eventually the dog lets go.

Walking home, Klara tries to link arms. Elya shrugs her away. He wants to postpone the wedding until after he returns from Lublin. Klara will be disappointed. Libka will be disappointed. But what's more important than business?

Elya in his bedroll now pictures the house he'll buy for Libka on Lubliner Street, the finest street in Mezritsh, tree-lined and paved with small stones. Below the kitchen, they'll have a cellar for keeping fish and ice.

Then he tries to imagine Libka's naked body but he's never seen a woman or a girl without clothes. Only baby Zusa. Once Rifka from behind.

If Ziv were awake, he'd be thinking of Libka too, but Ziv, snoring, thinks of nothing. He's dead to the world. He doesn't even dream. Only soft boys dream.

Frogs croak, crickets chirp, and insects buzz, while Elya, still sleepless, imagines Lublin and its tramlines. When the moon, as big as the lid of a stewpot, rises even higher and shines even brighter from behind the nearby wood, turning the treetops silver, he wants to wake his friends and almost does. Elya has never felt as hopeful or inspired. He only wishes Ziv and Kiva were more interested in commerce. Never mind, he'll make businessmen of them yet. They're advancing at a good pace, but it's up to Elya to keep them focused. He will, of course, happily give encouragement and advice. How lucky they are, warm and dry with plenty of food to eat, clean water to drink, brushes to sell, and each other to rely on. When he marries Libka, as Elya still believes he will, he wants his friends Ziv and Kiva at his side.

Elya's blanket is scratchy with twigs and chips of wood. He stands up, shakes it out. The feather-filled *shlofen* bag and inflatable rubber pillow, invented in 1876, has yet to make an appearance in Poland, though Kiva's fancy bedroll is a step in the right direction.

Instead of lying down again, Elya roots through his knapsack and extracts the notebook he has brought to record profit and loss. At the top of the page he writes, '*Elya Grynberg. August 28, 1907*,' which is, in fact, 30 Av. 5667. A day to remember.

Then he stops writing. So far they have spent nothing. What can he record? Then, before he knows it, Elya's writing something else. '*Fine roads. Excellent weather. Birds.*' Now why has he written that? He doubts Kiva's uncle would approve. '*The sights afforded by these regions seem to elevate us. Observed many flowers unknown to me,*' he notes. '*And birds.*'

He's already mentioned birds.

Feeling uneasy about these observations, Elya drops his notebook and pencil, then sinks exhausted into his bedroll. Behind closed eyes, he sees the road to Lublin rushing towards him as if he were travelling at speed in a carriage with four large wheels. He's hardly thought about shoes all day. Maybe once, when he noticed and disapproved of Ziv's flashy but flimsy footwear with indecently pointed toes, crimped tongues and buckles. Cheap modern shoes, purchased, no doubt, from his father's old rival, the Shoe Wolf of Mezritsh.

That's all in the past, Elya tells himself. Think of the future.

Every time he thinks about the future, Elya feels a whoosh inside like kerosene igniting. Finally he falls into a doze, little knowing that he will dwell upon this day of comparative happiness forever.

In the night, when everyone's asleep, Ziv shaves off Kiva's eyebrows.

V

On day two, having barely slept, Elya wakes early. The sooner they start walking, the better. Sleep fast. Eat fast. Walk fast. That's Elya's motto. Who knows, they may even reach Lublin by nightfall.

Then he thinks of a joke.

'*One morning, a young merchant like Ziv Nagelbach gets dressed, but while putting on his shirt, a button falls off. Picking up his shoe, the heel falls off. Lifting his brush case (because it's his turn to carry it) the handle falls off.*

Now Ziv's afraid to pee!'

Is it funny?

It is!

Elya feels a rush of confidence, good humour, enthusiasm. The stars overhead have disappeared and the sky is illuminated by the first rays of light. What could be more promising than the start of the day? Despite his restless night, Elya's full of optimism and energy. He's a young man with young ideas. He knows exactly where he's going and why. He cannot wait to get walking. In his mind's eye he sees himself, Kiva and Ziv, arms linked, striding down the road. Then he spots Ziv's half-eaten potato lying in the grass. He lifts it up. Dusts it off. Puts it back in their food store, which he now examines. Soup? Gone. Cheese? Gone. Eggs? Gone. Bread? Stale. He thought there'd be more left over. Still plenty of cooked potatoes and a sack of millet donated by Kiva's father. No reason to buy provisions on the road if they're careful. He counts and recounts their money, sorting through the coins until he locates his lucky German pfennig.

Examining their water flask and finding it only half full, Elya makes a mental note to stop briefly in the first village they encounter, which from his map appears to be the Village of Lakes, and seek out a well or water pump. These are the best of times, he thinks, fetching lake water in a bucket for washing. When he returns, his friends are still dozing and he sits down to wait. He waits and waits. When he gets tired of waiting he paces. He walks to and fro with his hands clasped behind his back like a *zeide*. Without noticing, he walks right over the ash surrounding their bedrolls which may or may not have contained the footprints of demons.

Kiva wakes eventually.

Not Ziv.

Ziv loves to sleep.

'Ziv,' Elya gently touches his shoulder. 'You're missing the best part of the day.'

Ziv turns over in his bedroll. 'One minute more,' he begs.

Elya shakes him harder.

Ziv sits up.

Slowly he stretches, gropes for his trousers.

Elya hands him his sock, but where's the other one? He's only brought a single pair. The heel of Ziv's shoe is loose and wobbling. A button hangs from his shirt. 'I hardly slept,' he grumbles. 'You kept me up.'

'Me? You slept like a log.'

'No one could sleep with you thrashing.'

'Yeah,' echoes Kiva.

How could this be? Elya's ready to argue, but decides to let it go. Where's the profit in arguing? Elya should be grateful he was even asked to accompany these two to Lublin. There are other boys in town that Kiva and his cousin Ziv know better. Why not the twins Yossel and Yankel?

'It was Ziv's idea,' Kiva tells him. 'You weren't our first choice. We couldn't take Yossel without Yankel. And Itzak's father said no. And Benesh's father said no, and . . .'

Elya picks up their precious brush case. Everything is going to be fine, he tells himself, once they're on the road. But Kiva must recite his prayers before they can leave. Using a good deal of their drinking water in his ritual handwashing, he fills his folding cup to the brim, pours half onto one hand and, while reciting the appropriate prayer, washes that hand. Then he repeats the ritual, washing the other hand. He does this three times using three cups of drinking water in all. Not only is this a waste of water, it takes forever. Finally he dries both hands on a dainty towel embroidered by Mindel with his initials.

Elya burns with impatience but determines to keep quiet. Nothing better than anticipation, he tells himself. How much less would he have appreciated setting forth if they'd done so without delay?

'Are you finished yet?'

'Almost.'

'Now?'

'Nearly.'

While Elya kicks at mushrooms in the damp grass, Kiva tries the latrine again and is again unsuccessful. Back at the campsite, he recites a prayer for putting on his shoes. The right shoe first because the right is more important than the left. When tying shoes, however, it's the left shoe first. Would Elya like to know why?

Elya suppresses a scream. He uses the leftover lake water to completely extinguish their campfire, stirring the ashes with his shovel, then looks up hopefully. 'All set? This is the order of the day. Walk hard and fast to Lublin. No detours or meandering. No looking at scenery or stopping.'

They laugh because they don't think he's serious.

It is already half past eight by Kiva's father's watch which has Roman numerals and runs thirty hours without needing to be rewound. Kiva winds it anyway. 'What about breakfast?' he enquires, wishing for something that isn't there.

'We'll stop on the road,' says Elya, although he has no intention of stopping.

Would he be in such a hurry if he knew what awaits them?

Probably not.

Don't hurry, Elya.

'Perhaps a drink of water,' Ziv suggests, filling his cup to the brim before drinking it down.

Then Kiva thinks he might need the latrine again, but instead of trying to do his business in the hole Elya's dug, he ventures into the woods for privacy.

Big mistake.

Kiva is sitting on a small mound in the woods with his trousers around his ankles trying to move his bowels. Spreading trees with stiff dark leaves hide the sun. He strains, panting.

Bowels must be opened every day. It is commanded.

He strains again.

He'll do himself an injury.

Then he hears someone approaching and peers into the gloom.

'Ziv?'

Not Ziv.

'Elya?'

Not Elya.

A beautiful woman is coming towards Kiva through the trees. How is it possible? He squints into the gloom, pulling up his trousers just in time. Then she's right in front of him and he sees it's his sister Mindel.

'Mindel, how did you get here? Did you follow me? Go home. You're not dressed right.'

As if she doesn't hear him, Mindel, wearing only a bedjacket, starts slowly undoing the buttons, revealing big breasts with rosy nipples and Kiva, watching, feels a stirring of desire. The woman coming towards him is not his sister. Too late he realises it's the demoness Lilith, spirit of darkness, uncontrolled female needs, and wet dreams. She wants to copulate with Kiva right here in the woods.

Copulate? The word dances in his brain.

Woe to those who are ignorant and therefore unable to ward off her advances, Kiva thinks, and starts reciting a prayer. She has, however, already got his *petzele* in her hands and is rhythmically stroking until it becomes as hard as a tree. Kiva tries, really tries, to entrust himself to the benevolent care and foresight of Adoshem, but the demoness is stronger. Her eyes turn red, her ears hairy. On her temples, foul black horns erupt; on her back, devil's wings; around her head, demonettes, small as mosquitoes, dance.

Looming over Kiva, she tears off his shirt.

Finding himself extended well beyond his natural size, stretched out on a bed of leaves, the demoness lying on top of him, Kiva moans, thick and low. And then, without willing or wanting, he enters her.

Kiva Goldfarb is copulating in the woods with a demoness. Perhaps he's been poisoned by ingesting grains, probably rye, infected with ergot fungus. His father the miller is known to be parsimonious. What he cannot sell, he feeds his family. Ergot poisoning most frequently occurs in summer, like this summer, following a cold, wet winter, like last winter, and a long damp spring, like last spring. Symptoms include muscle twitching, babbling, visions, trances, wild hallucinations and altered mental states. Convulsions may follow.

Moments later Kiva wakes covered in leaves. What has he done? He retches, vomiting pins. His belly large, his face yellow, his mind disturbed, he limps out of the forest, turning first in one wrong direction, then another. He hasn't even moved his *farkakta* bowels.

Meanwhile Elya and Ziv notice he's gone. And what of it? Elya is more than anxious to get going. Lublin beckons but what can he do? Kiva is nowhere to found. Last seen entering the woods alone.

Elya doesn't know if he's sorry or glad.

'He probably went home,' Elya says.

'You mean escaped?' Ziv says.

'Very funny. Anyway, he's gone.'

'He could have waited for me,' Ziv cries, taking his disappointment out on a young tree which he beats with his stick, while Elya gathers up his possessions and prepares to depart. 'Kiva wouldn't want us to linger. We're almost there,' he says.

Just then, Kiva stumbles out of the forest. Elya embraces him, guiltily.

'Where've you been?' says Ziv.

Kiva's mouth tightens.

'Well?'

'Picking berries.'

Kiva's face is mottled, his neck scratched, his pants on fire. He lowers his eyes and tries to forget. He's not prepared to tell. Not yet. Not ever. Not in so many words. Elya, who nearly abandoned him, so great his desire to reach Lublin, also tries to forget. 'Can we go now?' he asks.

They may have taken a while, but once ready, they're the best of friends. Walking three abreast, Ziv, in the middle, takes Elya and

Kiva by their necks and knocks their heads together. The air is fresh and cool, good walking weather without a hint of how hot it will soon become. Then Elya breaks away, hoisting his pack higher and higher, Ziv at his heels.

Kiva, however, is bent over studying the ground. 'Look at this,' he says. 'Is it not a miracle? Come. Observe.' He plucks up a small weed and regards the flat flowers sprouting in loose clusters along its stem with wonder. 'Like tiny, golden buttons,' Kiva marvels, professing himself content to study them for an hour, a lifetime, praising Adoshem and trying to find a way back into his good graces.

'And this?' Kiva takes up another even smaller weed. 'Look how the leaves clasp the stem.'

Elya wants to throttle him, but reminds himself they're friends.

Finally, they gather up their walking *shteks* and set forth in earnest. Elya is in such a hurry to get away, he forgets his shovel. Kiva forgets to bless their flask which causes it to empty quickly. Ziv forgets his purpose, if he ever had one.

'Lublin by nightfall,' shouts Elya. The road ahead fills his vision and he swings the heavy brush case he carries to indicate his determination. But no sooner do they take to the road, then they find themselves stuck behind a peasant with an ox-cart, proceeding at a snail's pace and impeding their progress.

'Hey big *tochus*,' Ziv hollers.

'Shush,' Kiva whispers. 'He'll hear.'

'Big arse,' Ziv yells again.

'Shush,' Kiva whispers again.

The peasant's dog walking beside the cart turns to snarl at them and Kiva falls back taking refuge behind Ziv. Soon there will be more dogs on the road, farm dogs, hunting dogs, watchdogs, strays, and packs. The only dogs Kiva approves of are Torah dogs said to protect the holy texts. 'I'll give any dog you don't like a thrashing,' Ziv reassures him. Grumpy from being woken too early, one hard shoe already rubbing one sockless foot, Ziv dawdles. He's come on this trip to sleep, grow a beard and make mischief. Not to walk for hours every day, longer and further than he's ever walked before. The road already appears endless, his boredom transforming it into something to be endured. But for Elya, the road's a joy, a short, swift route to attainment, although the summer sunlight falls equally on both of them, thus proving Albert Einstein's new and special theory: all motion is relative and the speed of light is always the same. This is something Elya's former best friend,

Mordy Peepzeit, tormented for his brains, his thick eyeglasses and trailing shoelaces, would have appreciated. But Mordy, if he's still among the living, is a conscript in the Tsar's army now and will have not a moment for relativity, special or otherwise. Addressed by his superiors with the familiar Russian 'you', normally used to address only children or animals, Mordy will have ceased regarding himself as a lad capable of thinking.

Elya, meanwhile, waits for Kiva. They walk together without speaking until Kiva lags behind again. Sliding a hand slyly into a pocket filled with sugared walnuts, he finds one and puts it in his mouth. Then another. He gets grains of sugar on his fine coat and brushes them off before anyone sees.

'I wish I had a coat like yours,' Elya says, waiting for him to catch up.

'Pray for one,' says Kiva.

It's not as early as Elya would have liked, but it's still early. The road, where very bad things will soon happen, shines with a violet hue. A fingerpost reads: LUBLIN 75 versts. And they all cheer.

Elya clasps Kiva to one shoulder, Ziv to the other. 'Good men,' he says. 'Glorious weather.'

'Getting too hot,' says Ziv, who cannot agree with any statement.

'Still pretty good. Be there soon.'

'Do you think?' Kiva brightens.

'It's not so far. And if we pick up the pace. Maybe tonight. Tomorrow at the latest. Look out. Horse dung ahead,' he calls to Ziv who's advancing from behind.

'That's not dung,' says Ziv, pushing ahead of him.

'What is it?'

'I don't know but it's not dung.' Ziv turns his long back on Elya and walks away. 'Are you coming or not?' he calls over his shoulder.

Meanwhile, Kiva finishes his sugared walnuts in secret. One left. A half. All gone. There are broad fields as far as the eye can see and Kiva wants to stop and pick wildflowers like a girl, but Elya urges him on. The sky's enormous, although Ziv's seen bigger.

When? In his dreams?

They stop walking to argue. Then Ziv needs another *pish*. He takes lazy aim at a bush, slowly changes his mind and picks out a hedge instead. Even the stream arching from his *pisher* is unhurried.

Overhead and far aloft, a great bird circles. It's brownish grey in colour with a wide chest and wedge-shaped tail, wings long and pointed. 'Will you look at that,' Elya says, squinting up towards the bright hot sky. The only birds he knows are *shtetl* birds, Mezritsher *foygl*, caged in courtyards, rustling on ledges, flailing against closed windows, trapped inside chimneys, tormented by young boys like Elya's brother Fishel.

One winter afternoon Fishel constructs a bird trap in the snow. First he scatters seeds on the ground. Over this, he props an old door on a big stick. Around the stick, he ties a length of rope. He holds the loose end and hides behind a tree. When starving little birds come to peck the seed, Fishel pulls the rope, dislodging the stick and bringing the door down splat.

When the door is lifted, blood and feathers.

Such a door might be said to hang over Mezritsh by those who can see into the future, like Elya's sister Rifka, who's such an embarrassment.

Meanwhile on the road to Lublin the great bird lands on the branch of a tree and the boys tiptoe closer. Suddenly it takes off, soaring and circling. Then, in a single, swift dive it grabs a smaller bird in flight.

'Did you see that?' Ziv cries, overcome with excitement.

Seized then released, the small bird tumbles to the ground, stunned but still alive. Then the great bird flutters after it, breaks its neck and carries it off.

But not far.

'Get out of the way,' Ziv shoves Elya aside, experiencing a thrill he cannot explain. 'I want to see.'

While Elya and Kiva hide their eyes, the *grosser foygl* drops the *kleine foygl* and begins plucking and eating it. Only Ziv continues to watch. He imagines possessing such a bird. 'What's it called?' he will ask the others. But no one will know. Perhaps an eagle.

Kiva must recite Kaddish for the small dead bird before they can set off again.

'After you,' Elya lets Ziv go first. But Ziv doesn't want to go first and lingers well behind to tease. And Kiva? Taking short, then even shorter steps, he cannot keep up, which provides Elya with another precious opportunity to practise patience. Patiently he allows himself to stop and admire the woodland around them, the dense brush and timber, the lattice work of leaves above their heads; then quickly promises the Uncle that he will cease stopping, cease admiring, and set to. He takes out his map and studies the route. The Village of Lakes cannot be far.

'Three travellers on their way to Lublin come across a pair of tracks and start discussing what sort of animal made them. One boy says bear, the other deer, the third fox. They stand there arguing, but before they can agree, they're hit by a speeding train.'

'That isn't funny,' says Kiva, who is sensitive.

'I thought it was funny-ish,' says Ziv, who is not.

Making no effort, sleeping as he walks, Ziv wakes up when he hears the sound of a wagon approaching from behind at speed. 'Do you dare me?' he calls out.

'Dare you what?' Elya turns around.

'Watch this.'

Leaving Kiva and Elya at the side of the road, Ziv runs into the middle where he stands tall, waiting.

'Nooo,' wails Kiva.

They can hear the wagon coming and soon it appears, horses flying, high wheels spinning, heading straight for Ziv who darts away at the very last minute.

The wagon misses him by Russian inches called *dyum*.

'Less than *dyum*,' Ziv insists.

'OK, *liniya*,' which is one tenth of an inch, Elya concedes, giving Ziv a hard stare. 'You could have been killed.'

'Less than *liniya*,' Ziv brags. '*Tocka*,' which is one hundredth of an inch.

'That's impossible,' says Elya.

'The driver cursed me,' adds Ziv proudly.

After wagon-dodging, he needs a drink. He takes a long pull straight from their flask, glug-glugging it down, then passes it to Elya. Although thirsty, Elya refuses. 'Some humble observations,' he says to his friends. 'Our water's running low. From now on only small sips until we reach the Village of Lakes.'

'Get stuffed, dung-face,' Ziv cries.

'Yeah,' echoes Kiva.

Ziv fills the tin cup he wears around his neck. Then Kiva lets Ziv pour him a full cup too. But oh, no, there's a fly in Kiva's drink and he must tip it out. It soaks immediately into the ground which is very dry.

Elya tries to appear undisturbed. Deciding, once again, to see the positive side of whatever he encounters, Elya must praise Ziv who is daring and quick, and assign value to all his accomplishments. 'I'm impressed,' Elya smiles stiffly, pretending to find Ziv's childish recklessness admirable. 'Thanks,' says Ziv, genuinely pleased. Kiva recites a mid-morning prayer, as Elya carefully checks and rechecks his map then folds it up again, spotless as the day it was drawn, and puts it back in his pocket.

Could they have passed the Village of Lakes without noticing?

Around the next bend, they see a large carriage stopped at the side of the road. A rear wheel has come loose and the hub needs resetting. The driver stands beside two great horses with plaited tails; behind him, a Polish gentleman with a proud neck. As the boys approach, the gentleman beckons, pointing to his carriage. 'You there. Jews. Yes you. Over here.'

'We're no wheelwrights,' says Ziv, who's good with languages and can converse in Polish and Russian. He starts to walk off, Elya and Kiva at his heels. But, hearing the sound of light female laughter, Ziv must have a look. Three young misses are standing a little distance from the vehicle. One for each of us, he thinks, then waits for his friends to join him. But Elya and Kiva have already been captured, and are kneeling underneath the carriage, supporting its weight, while the driver tightens the lynchpin that connects the wheel to the axle, and the gentleman looks on.

When Ziv's discovered, he's ordered to join his friends.

Ziv refuses and tries to run.

Caught by the scruff of his neck he's roughly shoved under the carriage alongside Kiva and Elya. 'Hurry up,' the gentleman commands. But the carriage is heavy and there's much groaning. A sharp wild smell. Someone has peed their pants.

At last the job's done and they struggle out.

The young misses regain their seats beside the gentleman in the carriage and the driver regains his box. Then the boys, sweaty, grimy and sore, watch as the vehicle speeds off, dislodging road grit and dried mud.

Elya stands looking after it. The trembling in his shoulders is spreading to his hands, which shake uncontrollably. He's trying to think of a curse grave enough for the so-called gentleman. '*May he die in his shoes'* is immediately rejected. He needs an ordinary *shtetl* curse, wishing sudden or unexpected death in a public place.

'*May a wagon wheel run over his skull?*' he says instead.

'Feh,' says Ziv, 'you call that a curse?'

'*May he sit on infected wounds with a bare bottom,*' Elya tries again.

'Now that's a curse!'

A curse is not an idle threat. Everyone knows someone who's been destroyed by a curse.

'*May his* putz *turn to kasha*' is Ziv's best effort.

Better than Elya's.

Then a coin is thrown from the rear of the carriage and Elya eagerly dashes forward to pick it up. Not so bad after all, he thinks.

'I'm going home,' wails Kiva.

'I'm not,' cries Ziv.

'But you said,' Kiva wipes his nose on his good handkerchief.

'Yeah, well . . . I changed my mind,' Ziv wipes his nose on his shirttails.

No parasite feeding off the sweat of his workers is going to make Ziv turn back now.

'What about me?' Elya's too distraught to wipe his nose and snot trickles down his upper lip. 'You'd just run out on me? Both of you?"

'No.'

'No?'

'We were going to leave a note.'

VII

Ziv, who's no longer thirsty, takes a sneaky drink or two because he can. Then he must stop for another pee. It's not his fault. Don't blame him. He's got catarrh of the kidneys. Ask anyone. Ask *Herr Doktor*. Ziv's piss is as green as *shav* which is sorrel soup. Sometimes made with spinach, chard or nettles. Better green than red, no? Kiva stands next to him and has one too. Kiva's piss is gold in colour, naturally.

'Can we go on to Lublin now?' says Elya.

'Of course,' Ziv slowly and carefully buttons his trousers.

'I'll carry that,' Elya reaches for the water flask.

'Maybe you can take my pack too.'

'Your pack? I've got my own to carry.'

'I stayed, didn't I?'

As they walk, Elya staggering under the weight of two packs, Ziv tells them about the great burden of the working man and the new world that's coming. 'We will rise up along with the workers of all nations. *Shvita!*' he cries. This, Ziv believes, is the future for the Jews of Eastern Europe. 'We'll be agents of great social change. Therefore, it's our responsibility to remain in the *shtetls*, not run away to America like so many others. Migrators,' he sneers, slowing down.

'Not me,' says Kiva. He's never going anywhere again.

'You?' Ziv pokes his cousin. 'You're only waiting for the Messiah to appear on Lubliner Street astride a white goat.'

'Donkey.'

'Goat.'

'Donkey.'

'What do you reckon your uncle pays his workers?' Ziv asks, his eyes small in the sun. Kiva doesn't know. He stands with his fine coat neatly folded over one arm, like a guest at a Lublin inn waiting to be shown the cloakroom, and shakes his head.

'*Drek*,' Ziv tells him. 'And the conditions are terrible.'

'What do you want, all should be equal?' Kiva cries, dropping his coat in alarm. Elya bends down to retrieve it.

'Yes. All should be equal,' Ziv says. He stops and looks back the way they've come. 'I should be organising the noble brush and bristleworkers in Mezritsh instead of journeying to Lublin with the two of you.' He's imagining himself stood on a kerbstone haranguing a crowd. Back in Mezritsh however, for all his big talk, Ziv would most likely be lazing around the marketplace with the other *luftmenschen* making prune eyes at any girl who passes.

'I thought you decided to stay. I thought no parasite was going to deter you,' says Kiva. Ziv points a long finger at him. 'What about you? What are you doing here anyway? Someone like you? Those brushes are constructed of pig's hair. Or didn't you know?'

This is an uncomfortable truth and no one really understands why Jews, forbidden to eat pigs or raise pigs, can make brushes from their bristles. 'Your rabbis only care about lining their own pockets. They're getting a percentage.'

'That's not true!'

'A pig remains a pig,' Ziv insists. 'No matter what they say. Purified by rabbis,' he scoffs. 'They should be ashamed.'

Relying on patience, Elya tries to ignore this dispute which would not be as tormenting if they were walking. Can't they walk and talk at the same time?

'Jews are not forbidden to touch pigs, the rabbis have always ruled. And parts of the pig such as the skin, once tanned or in the process of being tanned, and the hair, once shorn or in the process of being shorn, are allowed,' says Kiva.

Is this the best argument he can come up with? A talented young scholar reputed to have strong powers of reasoning, arguing and concentration, Kiva sits all day in the yeshiva where he studies, paired with another inky-fingered lad who rarely sees the sun. Reasoning together, they contemplate a passage from the Torah alongside commentaries on that passage from the Talmud, and commentaries on those commentaries from other sacred books, searching for contradictions small as a grain of *pilpul*. This hair-splitting examination should have sharpened Kiva's mind.

'Are you telling me that the processed parts of a pig are not a pig, *putz-kop*?' Ziv regards his cousin Kiva as one of the dim and privileged classes with his heelless slippers, embroidered towels and soft pillows.

'You better not let my uncle hear that language. Or see these,' Kiva points to the pamphlets and newspaper clippings from the *Workers' Voice* peeping out of Ziv's knapsack. 'He'll throw you off the team.'

Ziv ignores him. 'What do you have to say, chicken-ears?'

Elya doesn't want any part of this conversation. He pictures Kiva's uncle in his frock coat with his skinny legs and little paunch, signing the Letter of Credit he will bestow, when he, Elya, is named Merchant of the Year. He's already memorised the Uncle's whole catalogue. 'Blanket brushes,' he recites under his breath in order to calm and distract himself, 'shoe brushes, snow brushes, carriage brushes, hairbrushes, bottle brushes, beard brushes, baby brushes, travel brushes, street brushes, hat brushes, souvenir brushes, paddles set with bristles for cleaning, sweeping and beating on a large scale in factories and farms, and artist brushes made only from the best bristles, the so-called lilies.' He has an idea for a brush on a pole that extends like a telescope to reach high ceilings and walls. Maybe the Uncle will be interested?

'Your thoughts, egg-face?' Ziv enquires again. 'Shouldn't you be back home organising the chicken workers?'

'I was only assisting my mother.'

'You're a chicken worker,' Ziv taunts.

'No, I'm not. I'm a merchant.'

'You're not a merchant yet. You're a trainee. A scurrier. And once we're back home, you'll be a chicken worker again.'

Elya just sells eggs in the marketplace. But his mother and her chicken-rearing apparatus rise awkwardly in his mind.

'*A man runs to the doctor,*' says Elya who doesn't know what else to say. '"*Doctor, doctor,*" *the man cries, "you've got to help me. My wife thinks she's a chicken.*"

"*How long has this been going on?*" Herr Doktor *asks.*

"*Two years.*"

"*Two years?*" *exclaims* Herr Doktor. "*Why didn't you come see me sooner?*"

"*I dunno, we needed the eggs.*"'

No one laughs.

They frown at each other, but of course they're still friends. What's a friendship that's not been tested? 'If you're so dissatisfied on the road, why did you come?' Elya asks Ziv.

'To meet girls,' Ziv leers. 'I was bored. It was a dare.' Then he looks off into the distance. 'Maybe I'll find my no-good father and give him what for.' Although how Ziv'll recognise this *shiker*, whom he hasn't seen in years, is a concern. But when he does, Elya thinks, Ziv'll kill him.

'What about you?' Elya asks Kiva.

'My mother made me,' says Kiva, avoiding Elya's eyes.

'So that's it? That's why you've both come? Shame on you,' Elya gives them his most disappointed face. 'What about advancement? Salesmanship? Prestige?' According to Elya, Mezritsh employs three thousand bristleworkers, which is half of all the bristle-workers in Russia and Poland combined. 'Isn't that impressive? Aren't you proud? The Uncle produces beautiful brushes, does he not?'

'The Uncle doesn't produce anything,' Ziv scowls. 'His ill-paid workers produce the brushes he sells.'

'Without Adoshem, there would be no brushes,' Kiva adds unhelpfully.

'There are no brushes equal to Mezritsher brushes which are equal to the unequalled,' Elya says. 'Last year alone, the town sold half a million silver roubles worth of bristles.'

'And whose pockets do those silver roubles line?'

'The workers get their share.'

'All the workers get is tired and sick.'

According to Ziv, until recently, the brush and bristlemen of Mezritsh worked a twelve-hour day cleaning mountains of raw pig hair with iron combs, producing clouds of dust believed to be responsible for the high incidence of lung disease in the town.

'The workers are growing impatient,' he warns.

They're not the only ones, Elya fumes. 'Can't we walk and talk at the same time?'

Ziv ignores him. 'The first strike of the brush and bristleworkers in 1900 secures a ten-hour day, which is like a miracle,' Ziv lectures his dozy friends, may they learn something useful on this *farkakta* trip. The second strike in 1901 achieves little; the third, in 1906, involves Ziv in a big way. 'Long live the first of May. Fight for an eight-hour day,' he hollers until he's hoarse. The owners respond with a lockout lasting eleven weeks. Ziv stands among the crowd of striking workers waving a red flag. He reads aloud to them from a newspaper called the *Alarm Clock*. When the owners bring in strike-breakers, the brush and bristleworkers, including Ziv, throw eggs, tomatoes, stones. There are arrests, imprisonments. The rabbis speak out against the strikers. The strikers speak out against the rabbis. In the end, the owners are forced to recognise the trade union and there is a pay rise, but *buntochikes*, or rebellious workers, are blacklisted. In their place, it's rumoured, the owners are hiring girls.

'It's not as bad as the tannery,' Elya puts in.

At the mention of the tannery, they all shiver.

'Tell me how they do it.' Kiva's wide-eyed.

'You know how they do it,' says Ziv.

'Tell me again.'

'You'll get those dreams,' Ziv warns.

This is not a story for women, or soft boys. According to Ziv, who claims to know everything unpleasant that goes on in Mezritsh, who relishes tales of disgust and loves to shock, the decomposing animal flesh, fat and hair is removed in the tannery by soaking the raw skins in *pish* or painting them with slack lime. After which they're forked out and softened in dung, or soaked in a solution of animal brains.

Kiva squeals. And Elya forgets to be impatient.

Sometimes the dung is mixed with water in a *schissel* and the skins are kneaded for hours by hand, the poor workers swaying on their feet with exhaustion, slipping on slops as they move from one vat to another. And the smell!

Some workers lose hands, arms, feet to infection. Others develop tannery legs from standing long hours at the vats. Most pitiful are the shovellers, who clean out the traps where the gristle, scrap and solid grease collect, and then shovel it into the open sewers behind the works.

'Children play there,' Ziv complains.

Kiva turns pale. Is he going to be sick?

Any leftovers are boiled off to produce glue. Nothing goes to waste in the tanneries of Mezritsh except working men's lives.

Kiva blesses the tanners and their hides, the vat stirrers and their vats, the shovellers and their shovels, the scrapers, soakers, dung and water-pot collectors, the fleshers, dredgers, picklers, unhairers (also known as scudders), baters (don't ask!), scalders, degreasers, pounders, and dippers. This takes forever. Elya grits his teeth. Holds his breath. At last Kiva's done. Elya can breathe again. 'Let's go,' he cries.

'Wait a minute,' Ziv interrupts. 'What about the brushmakers and their brushes?'

And Kiva must bless them too.

'I need a drink,' Kiva gags when he's finally finished. And Elya stops pacing and passes him the water flask. Kiva takes a sip of warm water and spits it out. 'Tastes like bird water,' he complains.

The flask is even emptier now as the sun climbs towards noon. How is Elya ever going to get his friends to stop dawdling and start walking? 'Behold! Up ahead,' he motions towards a tiny blue and yellow bird poised on the bark of a tree. But Ziv has no interest in small birds. They glare at each other until Kiva makes them shake hands. He'll tell a story about birds if they'll all be friends. Kiva has many stories to tell. This one, the famous Parable of the Two Eagles, begins with an eagle landing on a cedar tree in Lebanon.

'Can't you find some real stories?' Ziv complains.

'This is real.'

'But is it true?'

'Of course it's true.'

Elya doesn't care if it's true or not, as long as they're walking.

'The eagle, which was sent by Adoshem to find a homeland for the Jewish people, breaks off the top shoot of the tree . . . '

'What's the purpose of that?' Ziv groans.

'. . . and carries it to the land of merchants.'

'Merchants?' Elya looks up with sudden interest.

'Babylon.'

'Babylon? Why Babylon? Why not Lublin? Or Leipzig?' Elya doesn't like associating merchants with Babylon, a place of wrong-doing. 'Eagles don't plant shoots.' Elya feels sure this is true although he cannot actually picture a real eagle. Or a shoot. The only eagles Elya knows are the double-headed eagles on Russian coins and banknotes. Shoots are a mystery.

'They don't need to plant them,' says Kiva. 'They just drop them on the ground and they flourish. But Adoshem's not satisfied. He sends in a second *grosser* eagle to drop a shoot in Egypt. But Egypt's not the right place either. So Adoshem dismisses the eagles and does the planting Himself in *Eretz* Israel.'

Everyone imagines a great finger reaching down from *Gan Eden* to designate a Jewish homeland.

Some other places, either recently proposed or soon to be pro-posed, as potential Jewish homelands include: Uganda in East Africa, the autonomous province of Oblast in Siberia, Alaska, and Madagascar.

No sensible person or nation wants Jews on their doorstep. *Farsteysh?*

'Why does He need eagles at all?' Elya asks. 'If He's Adoshem? Why doesn't He just plant it where He wants it to begin with?'

'Because,' says Kiva, 'He requires men to contemplate and ques-tion, as you are doing, to unravel His parable slowly. Bit by bit.'

'I'm not,' says Elya.

'Me neither,' says Ziv.

'The cedar is a symbol of righteousness,' says Kiva. 'And its bark is a cure for leprosy, if anyone is interested.'

No one knows what to say to that.

'Let's just not talk,' says Elya.

'Don't you believe in Adoshem and his miracles?' asks Kiva.

'There is no Adoshem,' says Ziv.

'You mustn't say that!' cries Kiva, who imagines Ziv roasted in Gehenna by demons who will hold him over the flames with laundry tongs.

'Was the great bird we saw an eagle?' asks Ziv.

'Yes,' says Kiva. 'King of *der foygles*.' But what does he know? The only time Kiva and his yeshiva friends have anything to do with *foygles* is when they chase swallows off the synagogue roof, because a swallow, it is said, carried in its beak the flaming piece of wood that started the fire that burned down the second temple in Jerusalem. All that's left is the Wailing Wall. One day, Kiva hopes to pray at this wall and slip a roll of paper, as is the custom, into one of the crevices between the old limestones. Kiva's prayer note will contain a plea for forgiveness.

'Please Adoshem . . . '

And?

That's Kiva's business.

His private business.

VIII

'All you can do is change yourself,' says Elya. 'You can't change the world.'

'Adoshem can,' says Kiva.

'Striking men can,' says Ziv.

They've stopped for lunch and are eating cold roast potatoes and stale bread by the side of the road under tall trees, though Ziv has seen taller.

Clouds of blackflies trouble them, mosquitoes and winged beetles, but no one can be bothered to move. When a female mosquito, its mouthpart adapted to sucking, lands on Kiva's arm, he stares at it transfixed. A fly swatter would have been welcome. Constructed from a square of wire mesh nailed to a wooden *shtek*, it's the most effective measure in the war against flies and the diseases they carry.

'When will people wake up?' Ziv asks the air.

This is amusing coming from Ziv.

'Men shouldn't worship wealth,' Kiva adds, which is also amusing coming from Kiva, with his gold watch and chain, his fine coat, and night shoes. 'I have these things,' he admits, 'but I don't worship them. They're not, and never will be, objects of veneration, as the prophet Elijah said to King Ahab.'

'Ahab?' Blank stares. More swatting.

'The evil ruler of the Kingdom of the Ten Tribes, who allowed the worship of Ba'al, and other idols.'

'Oh, that Ahab.'

Both Elya and Ziv groan.

'The prophet Elijah warned King Ahab that if this idol-worshipping continued, his kingdom would be tormented with *veytik aun tsores, tsores aun veytik*. But did Ahab listen? He took no notice and a terrible drought and famine came upon the land.'

'Who cares,' shrugs Ziv. 'Those who cry out against injustice in the workplace are the only real prophets.'

'Like you?' asks Elya.

'Yeah, like me.'

Ziv puts a whole potato in his mouth and chews rapidly.

Why can't he walk as fast as he eats?

'And what about you?' Ziv asks Elya. 'When will you join the workers' struggle? Chicken Workers Unite!'

'I told you. I'm not a chicken worker. When I save enough, I'm going to America.'

There it is. He's said it. He didn't mean to, but he has. A ship's ticket, earned with his own money, and he's on his way. Ed, Elya decides, he'll be called Ed in America. Or Eddie. First Lublin, where he'll sell many brushes, coming to the attention of the Uncle and securing a promotion. Then Lubliner Street in Mezritsh, where he'll have a fine house, then America, where every street is Lubliner Street. He dreams of the new coins he'll learn to tell apart and the new jobs he'll get, each one better than the one before, the ready-made suits, fedoras, and smart celluloid collars he'll wear, and the fair-haired American girls he'll encounter. In America, there'll be no blankets chewed by mice, no dusty bird cherry bushes, no women selling pins door to door.

'America,' Ziv scoffs.

'*Der Goldeneh Medina*', as it's called, is also the term used to convey a fool's paradise, a credulous hope that always ends in disappointment. According to Ziv, the Golden Land is a hoax invented by the Tsar and his minions to divert people from the real struggle. '*May you never reach America,*' he says to Elya.

This is the *Tata* of all curses for someone like Elya.

And Kiva agrees. 'There are no shuls or studyhouses there, only cowboys and gangsters.' Then Elya, battling a lump in his throat, stands and begins packing up, almost pulling his tarpaulin out from under them. But Kiva hasn't finished. 'I'm not finished either,' says Ziv, chewing more slowly. 'Can't I have another unsurpassed potato?' he asks with a smirk.

'Take it with you,' says Elya. He refuses to feel ashamed for wanting to better himself. Ziv tries another potato, but it's half raw and he tosses it into the long grass for Elya to pick up.

'Potato fight!' Ziv shouts and lobs one at Kiva.

Kiva lobs one back at Ziv.

'Hey! We might need those potatoes,' Elya sputters.

'All right,' says Ziv. 'Water fight!' He dumps most of what remains in their flask on Kiva, then grabs the last potato and stuffs it in his mouth.

You should choke on it, Elya thinks, and immediately feels sorry, then angry, then sorrier, then angrier. Shall we come to blows over a potato, he ponders, trying to dissolve his rage. But like the gristle, scrap and solid grease caught in the tannery traps, it will not dissolve.

'Your place is in Mezritsh, labouring with the chicken workers for justice and social change,' Ziv tells him, as he gets to his feet.

'Don't listen to him,' says Kiva. 'Your place is in Mezritsh working for the glory of Adoshem.'

'Chicken workers.'

'Adoshem.'

'Chicken workers.'

'Adoshem.'

And so they go on.

This is a joke Elya will not be telling:

'Two Mezritshers meet on a street in America. "How are you?" one asks.

"Not so good," the other replies. "Last month I spent on doctors twenty-five American dollars."

"Twenty-five dollars! In one month!" exclaims the first. "Back in Mezritsh you could have been sick for two years for that kind of money."'

The joke is complicated and ironic. His so-called friends would never get it. They don't have a feeling for the tragic quality of life. Elya, although he considers himself an optimist, understands misfortune. Now he's suffering the dead weight of a joke untold.

For all his jokes, he's really a serious lad. Klara remembers her son with a shoe brush, dutifully polishing. Or morosely rattling a noisemaker made of tin, producing a doleful grating sound on the joyous holiday of Purim when Jews are commanded to have fun. This is worth noting as it not only demonstrates Elya's gravity, but a certain self-consciousness even on a day of silliness, feasting and misrule. Purim, as Kiva would tell you, celebrates the accomplishments of the Jewish Queen Esther, who in ancient times outwits Haman, an evil advisor to the Persian king Ahasuerus. Haman is hatching a plan to kill all the Jews in the land. Imagine that! And he would have succeeded if not for Esther.

In the synagogue during the traditional reading from the Book of Esther, whenever the name 'Haman' is pronounced, the congregation grind their noisemakers to drown it out. 'Haman' occurs fifty-four times in the Book of Esther, giving some unfortunates, like Klara, headaches. Others write the name 'Haman' upon the soles of their shoes.

On the slow road to Lublin, they pass fields of grain not yet cut, a forest of white trees, no villages. Another *pish*? They stop so that Ziv can pee into a tangle of creepers. They should have arrived at the

Village of Lakes by now. Can they be walking even more slowly than Elya imagines? He must think of something to hurry them along. He studies his map with its roads indicated by thick lines, thin lines and broken lines, its mountains by tiny arrowheads. It's Ziv's turn to hold the brush case, but Ziv passes the case to Kiva, while Elya strides ahead. One last push, he thinks. We're almost there. But it's as if Kiva and Ziv are stuck on the road behind another slow and heavy ox-cart, a herd of meandering goats, or a procession of the old and infirm seeking a miracle rabbi to restore them. 'What time is it?' Elya asks, looking towards Kiva's watch with hungry eyes. He should be the one wearing the watch. He pulls Kiva to one side. 'I don't mean to alarm you, but I think we're being followed.'

'Followed! By who?'

'We have to hurry.'

'Cossacks?'

'Hurry!'

And Kiva hurries.

And seeing Kiva hurry, Ziv hurries.

Finally they're walking at a good pace. Not a bad idea, Elya.

'Accelerando!' he cries, striding forth.

'That's not a word,' says Ziv.

'It's a word.'

The road climbs steadily uphill and it becomes cooler and fresher. Elya shivers, pleasantly at first. Most delightful, he thinks as they ascend. Then, all at once, the distinctive smell of something baking wafts through the air, accompanied by the unmistakable whiff of warm sugar and stewed fruit.

'Prune Town!' Kiva exclaims, as if eating pastry were his only goal in life. He begs the others to stop. But Elya refuses out of spite, despite the fact that they need water and there must be a standpipe or a well in the town. And Ziv? Ziv shrugs. 'Where's Girl Town?' he enquires, unhelpfully. 'I thought we were stopping at Girl Town.'

'We can't stop at both,' says Elya.

'You promised,' wails Kiva.

'That was before we fell behind. You should have walked faster.'

Kiva is nearly in tears. 'Please,' he takes hold of Elya's sleeve. But Elya shakes him off, the promise of a prune pastry shrinking, then disappearing in stages before Kiva's eyes, from sugar-sprinkled lid to buttery base.

The ascent becomes steeper. In the distance, upland shepherds' huts are observed. Different birds fly overhead. There's a laughing bird Elya tries to imitate that has the others stopping up their ears, and one with a short, shrill, humming call that Kiva mistakes at first for the sound of a bullet whizzing past, taking cover when he hears it. Then the road, no more than a woodland track, begins to rise even more steeply. Trees with needles of the darkest green, giving forth an oily, sharp scent, press close, hiding a chilly sky and darkening the way.

At the sound of distant barking, Kiva looks over his shoulder. 'Did you hear that?' he asks Elya in a whisper.

'What?' Elya swivels around. 'I don't hear anything.'

'Cossacks,' cries Kiva, 'with dogs. Where's Ziv?' Kiva turns his head sharply this way and that. 'They've taken Ziv!'

Then Elya hears it too. Loud barking and growling, getting closer and closer.

Kiva clings to his legs.

Elya shakes him off.

'Run!'

Elya hides behind a clump of roadside bushes, leaving Kiva frozen to the spot. The growling and barking gets closer, louder. Elya digs his face into the dirt, while Kiva covers his head with his hands, closes his eyes and starts to recite the Shema, the prayer of the dying. 'Shema Yisrael . . . '

Then around the bend comes something padding softly in the dusk. It's Ziv, endeavouring to raise their spirits. He's on all fours, barking and howling and snapping his big teeth like an angry young dog.

'That wasn't funny,' Elya cries. He's bothered by the fact he's run away, leaving Kiva to fend for himself.

'Somebody can't take a joke,' Ziv jeers.

'A bad joke,' says Elya.

Ziv rolls his eyes.

'This trip is not an amusement. Think of the future. Don't you want to succeed in the marketplace?'

'I don't see a marketplace.'

'Forget it.' Elya walks away.

'What future?' Ziv calls after him. 'In fifty years, we'll all be dead.'

'Not necessarily.'

'OK sixty years. And this stupid journey of yours'll be meaningless.'

'It's not my journey. It's our journey.' Elya turns to face him.

Meanwhile Kiva sits down at the side of the road, takes off his glasses and wipes his wet eyes.

'Are you all right?' Ziv enquires. 'Have a sip of water.' He offers the near-empty flask as consolation. Then he helps Kiva up, takes him by the arm and leads him away. 'I'll look after you,' Ziv, his tormentor, promises. While Elya watches tight-jawed, they walk off together.

'You can be my armour-bearer,' Ziv lets Kiva carry his pointed stick.

Has Kiva forgotten Ziv's cruel joke already? Or is he angry with Elya for abandoning him in the middle of the road? Or for not stopping in Prune Town?

While Elya imagines fiery prune pastries soaring through Kiva's mind, Ziv voluntarily picks up the brush case (first time today), pretending to stagger under its weight, making Kiva laugh. Walking, talking and laughing together, they continue to exclude Elya, who, following behind (first time today), tries to listen in to what they say.

Soon Kiva and Ziv are walking at their snail's pace once more and Elya overtakes them. Is Ziv making faces behind his back? Whenever he turns around, Ziv, *may he piss dust*, is smiling.

'If you really want to know, we're talking about fleas. Kiva's got them!' Ziv jumps away from his cousin.

'Ziv does.'

'Kiva!'

'Ziv!'

They push and jostle each other. Kiva falls. Laughs. Gets up. Ziv sends him sprawling again. Kiva laughs again.

Elya walks on, fuming, then stops suddenly in his tracks, remembering his excellent purpose. The most important thing, the only thing, is to get to Lublin. Don't argue. Pacify. Then divide and conquer. Forget Ziv. Get Kiva on your side.

'Sorry,' he says, joining his friends. 'I'm far too keen. Maybe Lublin can wait while we take our time, see the sights, enjoy ourselves, stop at an inn, or catch a carriage.'

Kiva gives his arm a squeeze and smiles at him. Somehow, Elya manages to smile back.

Soon they arrive at a large fork in the road. Should they go left or right? Elya studies his map. No such fork is indicated. What should he do? Whatever he does, he must appear confident. Quickly he chooses the road on the right. It's better paved and looks as if it's seen the most traffic.

'Are we lost?' Ziv enquires.

He wants us to be lost, Elya thinks. 'Of course not.' He leads them forward, showing no signs of doubt. 'This is the unmistaken path.'

IX

By the time they stop walking, it's almost dark and they must make camp quickly. Elya and Kiva collect wood and start a fire together like the best friends they're destined to become, while Ziv pores over a Russian novel he's stolen from the Mezritsher Library, straining his eyes in the fading light. Getting comfortable, he pulls off his shoes without undoing the buckles. The pleasure of having his shoes off is intense. Then Kiva stops what he's doing to bless Ziv's discarded footwear. According to Kiva, demons are everywhere, even inside shoes.

There are demons in carriages pulled by horses, demon dogs, demons reading holy books (you must never leave a holy book open for a demon to read), demons found in mills and bakehouses feeding on wheat, demon shoemakers, demon merchants, demon doctors.

'Demon rabbis,' Ziv puts in.

'There are three categories of demons,' says Kiva, ignoring Ziv. 'Those who are angels; those who resemble humans and surrender to the Torah; and those who have no fear of Adoshem and are like animals.' Blessings dispel most demons, so Kiva continues reciting them.

Nursing his poor sockless foot, narrow and bony, rubbed raw by his cheap shoe, Ziv looks up. Not a whistle this time. A harsh sound but low, metallic. Kiva is thinking spurs. And spurs mean horses. And horses mean Cossacks, who'll chase them across fields and drag them into ditches.

Tonight, however, as before, the sound turns out to be birds. Birds whose songs jangle like spurs; whose calls resemble the snap and slap of a horseman's reins or swords swishing through the air.

'It could have been Cossacks,' says Kiva who is not easily calmed.

Ziv gets up and prowls around, checking the edges of their campsite so that Kiva can settle. He returns with reassurances.

Elya would have checked, but Ziv beat him to it. Now Kiva looks at Ziv with grateful eyes. Never mind, thinks Elya, at least they're not under attack. How can they be under attack from something that's not there?

Following the 1905 October Revolution, instigated, according to the Tsar, by Jews, there are 690 pogroms led by Cossacks. The Tsar waves his stick of state, embellished with a double-headed eagle, and pogroms begin.

'What's a Tsar's stick called?' asks Elya.

'His sceptre,' says Kiva.

'His *putz*,' says Ziv.

Tsarist pamphlets accusing Jews of trying to destroy Russia and her territories are circulated. One of the worst pogroms follows in the city of Odessa, where more than eight hundred Jews are torn to pieces, flayed alive, or beaten to death, their bodies left in the streets for pigs and dogs to eat. Elya shrinks away at the thought. Even Ziv shrinks away. Hiding in your own home is useless. Locking the doors, extinguishing the lights and crawling on the floor so you cannot be seen from the street, is useless. Running with children on your back is useless.

Is it time for a joke?

'A young lad,' says Elya, 'who perished in the Odessa pogrom, goes up to Gan Eden where he meets Adoshem and tells him a vitz. Not just any vitz. A pogrom vitz. But Adoshem is not amused.

"That's not funny," Adoshem says.

"I guess you had to be there," replies the lad.'

Ziv and Kiva wait grim-faced for the punchline.

That was the punchline. Don't they get it?

They don't get it.

'That's not funny,' says Kiva, just like Adoshem.

Another subtle and irreverent Jewish joke bites the dust.

Recently things have calmed down. No Cossacks in tall sheepskin hats and black tunics ride through Jewish cities, towns and villages. Not these days, Elya thinks foolishly. No one he knows has ever even seen a Cossack.

Kiva's sister Mindel has seen a picture of one in a book, catching Jews like flies. Her fear of Cossacks often brings *zaftig* Mindel with her big knees and *grosser tochus* into Kiva's bed at night. But no one's to know.

When you baptise a Jew, the Cossacks say, hold him under the water for five minutes. Who, us? Elya thinks. Why us? We're just like everyone else, only maybe a bit more so.

After his fright, Kiva, with his chronic intestinal stasis, reckons he just might need the latrine. But, oh no, Elya cannot find his shovel.

'Perhaps you mislaid it,' Kiva suggests.

'Or perhaps,' says Ziv 'you left it home. Did you leave it home?'

'Of course not. I used it to dig our first latrine,' Elya says, searching.

'What does it look like?' Ziv offers to help.

'A small shovel with a short handle and a square point.'

'How can a point be square?'

'A square head, all right?'

It occurs to Elya that Ziv might have taken it.

Somewhere, but not on the road to Lublin, criminal investigators have discovered fingerprints as a method of apprehending villains and solving crimes.

'If it were not your shovel, but our shovel, commonly owned, it wouldn't be lost,' says Ziv. 'Someone would have looked after it. I would have looked after it.'

'You would have hit something with it. A helpless animal, or a young tree.'

'Whatever collapses from a shovel's blow, is not worth preserving,' proclaims Ziv. 'Down with private ownership!'

In Belgium, King Leopold II has recently claimed the African Congo as his private possession. But who knew? If Ziv knew he would have mentioned it.

'Adoshem can find your shovel,' comments Kiva. 'If you ask him.'

'Maybe it's here and you're just not seeing it,' Ziv smirks. 'Or maybe it walked off. A self-propelling shovel. It'll be in Lublin waiting for us.'

'Never mind,' says Kiva. The urge has gone.

'You're too attached to objects, you and Kiva,' observes Ziv. 'To desire nothing is to have no vulnerability.'

'It was a good shovel,' Elya insists.

'A good Jewish shovel,' says Kiva.

Ziv bats him fondly about the head and ears. Then not so fondly. After that, he bats Elya.

'Not the ears,' cries Elya.

As if through a pane of glass, Elya sees the riverbank where he lost his keen hearing. Was it only last summer? No, the summer before that, when, despite protests, the bathing places along the Krzna River in Mezritsh are opened to both men and women. Immorality is predicted. Ziv predicts fun. He has a plan to get the girls who swim there to notice him and Elya. 'We'll hide in the bushes and watch them,' he tells Elya.

'We're too tall for bushes,' Elya protests.

'We'll crouch down. Those bushes are high enough.'

'The ones with the prickles?'

'What are you, soft? Or maybe you're chicken? Chicken,' he calls out so loudly that anyone listening might hear.

'They'll still know we're there.'

'So what? They'll like it. Libka'll be there and Faigel and Fruma. Those girls swim in nightshirts,' Ziv's saying. 'And when they get wet you can see everything. Breasts,' he urges. 'Well?' He snaps his fingers in front of Elya's face. '*Vas mahkhsta?*'

Why, Elya's wondering, has Ziv asked him when he could have asked Yossel, or Yankel, or Kiva to the riverside? He's flattered and confused. Ziv has stolen a bottle of medicinal schnapps from the hospital where his mother works and they both take a sip. 'That's horrible,' says Elya. But Ziv pretends to like it. Then Elya pretends to like it. He draws on the cigarette Ziv hands him and feels dizzy. Then he tells a joke.

'*A poor man, who believes he's cursed because his son doesn't know how to drink or play cards, goes to see the rabbi.*

'*"That's not a curse," says the rabbi. "That's a blessing. Why are you complaining?"*

'*"Because he drinks and plays cards."*'

'I don't get it,' says Ziv.

When he gets it, he doesn't find it funny. Ziv's not a fan of comic sorrow. Ziv would like a joke that's funny.

When they reach the riverside, they find the bushes, not as large as Ziv promised, and pricklier. The girls in their long, thin costumes shriek when they see Ziv and Elya, but soon lose interest. 'Hey,' Ziv calls out. 'Watch this.' He does headstands on the grass while the girls ignore him. Elya wants to go home but Ziv drags him up to some rocks near to where the girls are sitting.

'I'm not diving here,' says Elya.

'What's wrong with here?'

'It's too shallow.'

'Nah. You're a good diver. And the girls'll notice. It's the reason I asked you.'

'Well, I can't do it,' Elya says.

'What are you, impotent?'

Elya has never heard this word before. But it must be a bad one. He takes off his shirt and puffs out his skinny chest.

'I knew you'd do it.'

Elya stares hopelessly down into the murky water. At the start of summer, the water's crystal clear. So clear you can see gudgeons below the surface. But by August, it's turned brown and scummy with a thick, oily consistency, like swimming in kerosene.

'You're not allowed to dive there,' the girls call out.

'They're watching,' Ziv cries, pushing Elya forward. 'Now go!'

This command is the last thing Elya will clearly hear. Despite his better judgement, he leans forward, feet together. He knows as he takes off that the dive isn't right. He hits the surface badly, sinks down, scrapes the side of his head and emerges, ears full of water. Ziv jumps in after him and holds Elya's head under with the playful intention of drowning him, while the girls look on. They start shrieking when Elya doesn't come up. Finally, Ziv lets go and Elya rises, gasping for breath, more water in his ears.

Elya used to be able to hear mud freezing, coats buttoning, cigarettes smoking, but diving into the Krzna River two summers ago has permanently damaged his ears. Paradoxically, his useless ears, already large, seem to grow larger and further from his head every day.

There's no best part of this story. Elya should have stayed home. He never wants to see Ziv again. But here they are together on the road to Lublin.

In the fire Elya builds, they toast millet cakes made with grain donated by Kiva's father. Kiva has jam and Ziv has an appetite. He may claim not to be attached to objects, but he's attached to millet cakes. 'Bestow another one upon me,' he requests with a smile. His smile is so genuine, so appealing, even Elya forgets to be irritated. Not such a bad fellow, he finds himself thinking. He hasn't given up on Ziv. Not yet anyway.

The air is even colder after dark and a damp chill rises up from the ground. Elya piles more wood on the fire. Soon the flames are so high they might be seen from the road. This makes Kiva uncomfortable. 'We don't want visitors,' he says, blinking smoke from his eyes.

Kiva and Ziv put on their coats, but Elya has not brought a coat. When his mother offers his father's greatcoat, stored in naphthalene and smelling strongly of it, he declines. Now poor Elya can't get warm. He shivers ostentatiously, hoping Ziv, who proclaims the common ownership of all things, will share his coat. But it doesn't occur to Ziv to offer. With no coat to put on, Elya climbs miserably into his bedroll, which he has moved closer to the flames. Never again will he complain about being too warm. He peers into the fire where for a brief moment he thinks he sees his shovel head melting.

Ziv picks up his book and attempts to read by firelight.

'What's it about then?' asks Kiva.

'Murder,' says Ziv. 'This young lad kills this old woman and her sister with an axe.'

For a while, no one says anything, then Ziv puts down his book and starts to tell his friends about his hero, Abe Attell, Featherweight Champion of the World, 1906. Ziv has his own boxing gloves and a striking bag at home. One day he is going to be a champion boxer. And a champion *shtupper*.

Elya isn't interested but feigns interest to please Ziv. Listening with painful concentration, he smiles. He can't help it. Deep down inside, Elya wants to be everybody's friend. Encouraged by Elya's interest, Ziv shows him a picture, cut out of the *Mezritsher Daily*.

Unfortunately, it has been so frequently handled the ink has smudged and the tiny Jewish-American prize fighter in his big padded gloves is barely recognisable. Later, 'The Little Hebrew', a suspected middleman for the gangster Arnold Rothstein, will be accused of fixing fights, using drugs and putting chloroform on his boxing gloves to temporarily blind his opponents. But for now he's a hero.

Dancing backwards and forwards on his feet, Ziv asks to be punched, there, right there. He points to his hard stomach. But Kiva punches like a girl. And Elya, although tempted, refuses. Then clever Ziv tries to swallow his walking stick for their amusement, point first. By turning his profile to Elya and Kiva, opening his mouth wide and pretending to feed the *shtek* down his throat, he delights them, pressing it close to the side of his face that's hidden from view. It's a good trick. They know what he's doing, of course, but it looks so real, Kiva squeals.

Now what?

'I have a story,' says Kiva. 'A true Jewish story.'

'Not again,' Ziv scoffs.

'I'd like to hear it,' says Elya, who wouldn't but determines to listen anyway.

Ziv reaches for his book.

'There are axes in this story,' Kiva tempts him.

'Axes?'

Ziv is tempted.

Then Kiva tells the story of his hero, Solomon, King of the Jews, and his nemesis, Asmodeus, King of the Demons.

'King Solomon desires to build a great Jewish temple in Jerusalem,' says Kiva.

Ziv groans.

'But the Bible tells us that a *grosser* temple must not be built with hammers, axes, saws or any tool which might also be used to destroy human life. What can Solomon do? Asmodeus gives Solomon the solution. "There exists in your kingdom a magic worm the size of a grain of barley," he says, "which can cut through stone with its teeth, like the blades of a saw."'

'Teeth like saws?' Ziv ceases groaning and puts down his book.

'Why would he tell King Solomon a thing like that?' asks Elya.

'He's Solomon's prisoner so he's willing to trade for his freedom. How Solomon captured that *gonif* in the first place is another good story.'

'Involving fighting and bloodshed?' Ziv asks enthusiastically.

'Involving drunkenness,' says Kiva. 'Later I'll tell that one.'

'Later when?'

'Don't you want to hear this one?'

'Yes, please,' Ziv gets on his knees pretending to beg, but is also really begging, and Kiva continues.

'Where will Solomon find such a rare and talented worm?' he asks.

Ziv leans forward, hanging on Kiva's every word.

'It can be found dwelling with a woodcock and its young.'

'What's a woodcock?' asks Ziv.

'A bird who has taken an oath to guard the worm.'

'Yeah, but what kind of a bird?'

'Birds eat worms,' comments Elya. He cannot help himself. The story is ridiculous.

'Really?' shrugs Kiva.

'What's a woodcock look like?' asks Ziv.

But Kiva doesn't know. Nor Elya. King Solomon must, because he sets out to find one. How Solomon locates the magic worm in the woodcock's nest is yet another good story Kiva will tell someday.

'When?' Ziv asks, the idea of a worm who resembles a saw tumbling through his brain.

'Tomorrow,' Kiva promises.

'Tomorrow's the story of drunkenness,' Ziv reminds him.

'The night after that,' Kiva promises.

'We'll be in Lublin by then,' says Elya.

'Who's your hero?' Kiva asks him.

'Don't have one.'

'But it's your turn.'

'Leave him alone,' says Ziv, 'he's missing his shovel.'

'You can have one of my heroes,' Kiva offers.

But Elya shakes his head. He has a hero, but he doesn't want to say.

'Yossel could have told a story about his hero,' Ziv complains. 'Or Yankel.'

Yossel, who'll jump from the cattle car of a speeding train one day leaving Yankel inside, is a great storyteller. As is Yankel. Too bad they aren't here, and Elya is.

'How about a joke?' says Elya.

'Another *vitz*? Spare me,' says Ziv.

'As long as it's funny,' says Kiva.

Elya is saving his funniest jokes for Lublin. He tries to think of one that is good enough.

'*Once a poor shoemaker sells a tin of expensive English shoe polish. Next day the customer comes back with the tin. "Nisht gut," the customer complains.*

"Consider yourself lucky," says the shoemaker.

"Lucky? Why lucky?"

"I bought five dozen."'

Neither Ziv nor Kiva laugh. It's an old joke. Not the right joke.

'Even I can tell a better *vitz* than that,' brags Ziv.

'Go on then,' says Elya.

Big mistake.

X

'A rich man like Kiva's uncle orders a camel from Palestine,' says Ziv. 'He rides his camel around the marketplace and through the streets of Mezritsh, but eyn tog the camel runs away or is stolen, and Kiva's uncle offers a large reward for its return. Menschen come from far and wide to try and find the Uncle's camel.

"How tall is this camel?" they ask.

"A good ten handspans from the ground," the Uncle replies.

"And what colour?"

"Camel colour, of course."

"Male or female?"

"How should I know?" the Uncle splutters. "Wait a minute, I just remembered. It's a male. Every time I ride it through the marketplace, I can hear people yelling, 'Look at the shmuck on that camel!'"'

It's really funny. It might be the funniest joke Elya has ever heard. But he refuses to laugh. Instead, his eyes well up with tears and his nose prickles. Kiva, however, is laughing, although he knows he shouldn't. 'Kiva's got a *shmuck* between his legs, after all,' cries Ziv when he hears his cousin laughing at a rude joke. Then they both look at Elya who is still blinking back tears. 'It's your turn again,' says Ziv. 'You have to entertain us with something.'

Elya takes a moment. He needs a moment. 'How about money?' he says at last, trying to explain the rate of exchange because it's one of the most interesting things he knows. It's not a story or a joke and it doesn't involve a hero, but it's true.

'How about the life of a banknote?' Elya describes a Russian paper rouble, Tsar Nicholas II in profile on one side.

Ziv hates the Tsar. He claims never to have seen a banknote, although he'd like to see one and set it alight. 'Down with banknotes!' he cries.

What about gold? Are they interested in gold? Even gold doesn't interest them. What's Elya doing with boys who aren't even interested in gold? They jostle and elbow each other while Elya's speaking, Ziv locking his arms around Kiva's neck and Kiva struggling in his grasp.

'You must have a hero,' Ziv complains. 'Who is it?'

'It's the Uncle,' Elya says at last.

'*Der Feter*? Kiva's *feter*? That's a joke, right?'

'He's a self-made man, an inspiration to all, an example of what can be accomplished with focus and determination.'

'He's not very nice,' says Kiva.

'He doesn't have to be nice.'

'He's ruthless,' says Ziv. 'He squeezes his creditors, double-crosses his friends, ruins his rivals, exploits his workers. And he has a *kleine putz*.'

'How do you know? I think he has a *grosser putz*.'

'*Kleine*.'

'*Grosser*.'

'And he's mean,' adds Kiva who's seen him in his bristleyard checking the ground for stray hair.

'He's your uncle.' Elya looks at Kiva with pleading eyes.

Then Ziv takes up his book once more, tipping the pages towards the firelight. But he can't concentrate. All Ziv can think about is Kiva's magic worm, its teeth like a ripsaw tearing into stone. At first, he has trouble picturing it. The only worms Ziv knows are *shtetl* worms: earthworms, hookworms, pinworms, tapeworms and flukes; worms that eat raw leather in the tannery and corpses in the cemetery. But a magic worm would be nothing like that. Not grovelling or creeping along like an ordinary worm, not eyeless, damp-smelling fish bait. A broad and expansive worm, an unobstructed worm, inserted into Elya's bedroll!

In Vienna it's rumoured that rich *froys* swallow worms to lose weight. These worms live in their *kishkas* ingesting part of whatever they eat and growing long, longer than the road to Lublin, Kiva's prayers, or the brush for washing ceilings invented by Elya with its telescopic handle. In his mind, Ziv stages a series of fights. Eagle versus magic worm. Magic worm versus Cossack. Cossack versus eagle. Elya stages a fight between the Uncle and . . . well . . . who? The Little Hebrew? King Solomon? Stiff with cold, Elya can no longer feel his hands or feet. He gets as close to the fire as he dares, scorching his face and wishing for his father's old coat. From somewhere deep in the woods, an owl screeches. 'We have to have a scary story now,' Ziv remarks, 'because we're all alone, miles from anywhere, surrounded by a dark wood where men lurk who are not men but beasts like Mister Bristle.'

'Who?'

'Have you never heard of Mister Bristle? Has your mother never warned you? Your father? Perhaps they were too frightened to ever speak his name. Many knew him once upon a time as Shmuel Plattuck.' Ziv looks at his friends meaningfully, but says nothing more.

'Well?'

'Well what?'

'Are you going to tell us about him or not?'

'If I tell you, you won't sleep.'

'Nothing'll keep me awake,' says Elya.

'Or me,' says Kiva.

'We've walked miles.'

'Miles and miles.'

'If you're sure?' Ziv looks carefully over his shoulder before he begins.

'Shmuel's an ordinary bristleworker from Mezritsh. Then one day, he's fired for so-called slacking and forced to face starvation or take employment in the tannery as a shoveller. And you know what happens to shovellers don't you? They slip and fall head first into the vats for soaking hides. Usually they drown and have to be fished out with a hook.'

Kiva screams. 'Is this what happens to Shmuel?'

'It is. And when he climbs out . . .'

'He climbs out?' Kiva screams again.

'His eyes are gone.' Ziv rolls his own eyes back into his head so that only the whites are showing. 'His lips are black with dog dung; his skin red and raw from soaking in the *pish* of kerosene drinkers. And all over his body, hair as sharp as needles has grown. After that he runs away.'

'Where? Where does he go?'

'He *shlofens* one night in your father's mill.'

'No!' Kiva cries out.

'Of course he doesn't,' Elya nudges Kiva. But Kiva only glares at him.

'Then he takes to the road.'

'Isn't he blind?'

'He steals eyes, *shmuck*.'

'From who?' asks Elya.

'From *bokhers* like you and Kiva,' Ziv mimes popping an eyeball into his mouth, chewing and swallowing.

Kiva screams even louder, his own eyes shining with love for Ziv.

'And not only eyes. On the road he develops a taste for soft and oily human flesh.'

'Oily?'

'Well, wet, with all the blood that comes out.' Ziv puts his head on Kiva's shoulder and starts to gnaw. 'Whatever he doesn't eat, he'll fling to his dog.'

'He has a dog?'

Kiva's terrified, but Elya thinks it's amusing. He imagines a walking scrub brush, such as those that feature in the Uncle's catalogue with stiffened hairs.

'He might have followed us from Mezritsh,' Ziv stretches out the skin of his face pretending to be Mister Bristle, and for perhaps a moment appears not to be Ziv.

Kiva screams and laughs.

'He'll skin you alive,' warns Ziv, 'soak you in a vat of piss, stretch you on a wooden frame, then turn you into a satchel, a lampshade, a belt, or a bookmark. He might roast you like a chicken and gather up the drippings to spread you on a slice of bread. Or he can swallow you whole if he wants. Sometimes he'll only take the feet. A boy will have to walk on stumps.'

They all try to imagine that. Mister Bristle with his little bristle moustache, chasing Jewish lads who run in every direction, knocking each other down in their haste, cowering and sobbing. Elya shivers mightily but it's only because of the cold.

'Have you not heard him moaning?' Ziv enquires. 'Perhaps you thought it was the wind. Maybe you can hear him now?' And with that, he jumps up and starts strangling Kiva, who screams with terror and delight. Later Ziv will creep up behind Elya and touch the back of his neck with a hairbrush. Never have they had so much fun, Elya included. 'Maybe Mister Bristle took your shovel,' says Ziv, teasing him again.

'Why would he need a shovel?'

'He was a shoveller, *putz*.'

'There is no Mister Bristle.'

'Yes there is.'

The real Mister Bristle, according to Ziv, is Kiva's uncle, devouring his workers.

'He does have a big appetite,' Kiva admits.

The first time Elya encounters him, the Uncle is in his covered carriage, so long and wide it's become stuck along an insufficient street. Joining a crowd of onlookers, Elya stops to gawk. An old man peers out from one of the carriage windows, his expression remote. For a moment, Elya thinks it's the Tsar himself. He bows, goes down on one knee, feels stupid. He's the only one.

'It's the Uncle,' people cry.

A wealthy brush manufacturer named Velvel Goldfarb, the Uncle wears a sash from collar to hip, like the real Tsar, and is said to be so rich, he's visited by the butcher every day. His rise to fame from humble origins begins when the owner of one of the largest brushworks in Mezritsh goes bankrupt and *der Feter* acquires the business. A genius in commerce, finance and speculation, the Uncle expands, accumulating a very large fortune. Renowned for his cold intelligence, he makes his creditors weep.

Traversing Mezritsh in his magnificent carriage, the Uncle's feet never touch the ground. Or if they do, a carpet is laid on the mud for him to step on.

Wherever he goes, he's accompanied by a man with a hefty build who could have been a water carrier or a heaver of some sort, but is, in fact, his bodyguard. Since the strikes by turbulent bristleworkers who have formed an illegal Bund, the Uncle needs protection. He waves from the window of his carriage, and Elya feels light-headed, as if he's inhaled the gas for cooking recently installed in *Herr Doktor*'s kitchen. Only ten at the time, Elya raises himself on the tips of his toes so maybe the Uncle will notice him.

*

Before settling down for the night on the road to Lublin, Elya counts the leftover millet cakes. Later, in his bedroll, mosquito bites are driving him crazy. He lies on his stomach. Then on his back. He thinks of his shovel, its head shining in the moonlight. Except there is no moonlight. Or shovel. Only darkness and smoke, swirling and drifting from the dying fire and causing his eyes to water.

Meanwhile, crouched in his bedroll, Kiva's silently praying. Petitioning on behalf of his friends, Kiva asks Adoshem to help Ziv to find a magic worm, and Elya to find Lublin. And for himself? He asks only to wake up tomorrow morning in his own bed in Mezritsh, a puff of white sheets around his face.

Poor Kiva awakes not in the morning or in his own bed but in the middle of the night screaming, which rouses Elya who wasn't sleeping anyway.

Kiva dreams he's soaking like a hide in a tannery vat. Every time he tries to get out, a dog barks and the foreman pushes him under with a stick. The soaking *wasser* gets in his mouth and up his nose and tastes like over-salted kasha.

'It's just a dream,' Elya tries to tell him.

'Yeah but it felt real.'

'You're getting upset over nothing.'

'Yeah but maybe it was a message.'

'What message? From whom?'

Kiva says he doesn't know. But he knows. The message is from Adoshem. Punishment is coming for Kiva's transgressions. He coughs, then spits delicately into a handkerchief. Eventually he dozes again, cradling his walking stick in his arms. On his pillow next morning there's a spray of blood so fine it can hardly be seen.

It's very dark. The moon hasn't risen. Perhaps it will never rise, or perhaps it has risen but is hidden behind clouds. Elya hasn't slept for the cold, for Kiva, for thoughts that race around his head, for Libka, and Lublin, and Mister Bristle. He looks towards the woods but can see only darkness. In the darkness he thinks he can hear the brush, brush, brush of Mister Bristle's footsteps as he draws near.

'Ziv,' Elya calls out, 'stop fooling around.'

But Ziv's in his bedroll snoring.

Trying to regain the simple happiness he felt only yesterday, Elya looks hopefully at the sky. Searching deep inside his knapsack, he finds the prune pit Libka once sucked and the slip of paper on which he has written her name. He holds both items gently remembering. Then he gets up. The ground is damp. He stamps his feet, which are numb, and feels for his shoes. Someone has filled one shoe with salt for amusement.

'We might need that salt,' he cries, disturbing no one.

The suitcase that contains their brushes is a beautiful and distinctive object. Elya now kneels before it and runs his hands over the smooth leather to reassure himself. In a mountain of suitcases, Elya could easily locate this one. Then he opens it. He cannot explain exactly what he's doing or why. It's too dark to see anything clearly, so when his fingers touch something soft inside, for one terrible moment he thinks their paintbrushes have turned to ash or dust. Then he realises – moss litter. Gently he lifts this protective covering. The brushes lie in neat, ordered rows like sleeping children. Reaching for one, as if to rouse it, he brings it close, stroking the bristles lightly across his face. It smells inexplicably briny, also woody.

'Not long now,' he tells his brushes.

XI

Next morning Ziv jumps up ready to go.

In Elya's dreams.

Does he always sleep this late? He does. 'I get sick if I get up too quickly,' Ziv complains as he slowly staggers to his feet. 'Hold on. I can't see. Everything's spinning.' He lies down again and closes his eyes.

'Ziv are you all right?' Kiva cries.

'Of course he's all right,' says Elya.

Elya could have walked versts while Ziv – *may a fire burn in his shoes* – finally climbs out of his bedroll and reaches for his *matkes*, his *gatkes* and his trousers. 'I'm ready,' he says, half-dressed.

'You're not ready.'

'I'm almost ready.'

Elya picks up their precious brush case. The handle is slack. Has Ziv been releasing the screws? Elya wouldn't put it past him. Luckily, he has a screwdriver. After fixing the handle, he fixes his hair. Then Ziv comes up behind him and musses it. Then Ziv has a joke. Another joke?

'Three friends sleep side by side under the stars,' says Ziv.

'Like us,' says Kiva.

'In the morning the lad on one side wakes up. He's had a terrible dream. "Someone was trying to pull off my shlong," he says.

"I had the same dream," reports the lad on the other side.

"What about you?" they ask the lad in the middle.

91

"Me?" he says. *"I dreamed I was skiing."'*

Kiva laughs along with Ziv. He can't help it.

'Jews don't ski,' says Elya with a straight face.

'I didn't say they were Jews,' says Ziv.

'Yeah,' says Kiva.

Taking out his mirror in order to practise various dissatisfied expressions, Ziv turns to Elya. 'Want to see yourself?' he asks.

Is it a trick? Presented with Ziv's mirror, Elya ducks his head, shy of his own reflection. It isn't a good mirror and as he turns it this way and that, his features ripple and bulge, Elya with his father's nose and his mother's narrow face, his hair mussed, his cheeks grey from wood ash, his ears large as the ears of a demon from which hair is protruding.

'Give it back now,' Ziv glares at Elya.

'In a minute,' Elya glares at Ziv.

Both glare at Kiva, who sneezes.

Suddenly they're all jostling, pushing, running, screaming. Ziv's brought a ball.

'There's something I have to say,' Elya says, panting after kicking, throwing, catching, heading and bumping the ball with his *tochus*. 'Fellows,' he begins. Then hesitates, unsure of how to continue.

'Well?' Ziv shifts impatiently.

Ziv, impatient?

'We're having a wonderful time, are we not?' Elya begins again. 'But it has come to my attention that neither you Ziv, nor you Kiva, have assigned proper value to this endeavour.'

Ziv screws up his face. 'What do you mean, endeavour?'

'Trip.'

'Why don't you just say trip?'

'All right, trip. I know you want to take your time, have fun,' a grimacing smile, 'see the sights. But I also know, because you told me, that you have better things to do back home. We all have better things to do back home,' he adds insincerely. 'Why drag it out? The sooner we get to Lublin, the sooner we can return to Mezritsh.'

Ziv looks at Kiva.

Kiva looks at Ziv.

They both laugh.

Why are they laughing? Earnestly Elya presses on. 'This is the order of the day: brisk walking. *Farsteysh?*' He searches their faces for compliance. Brisk sneering from Ziv. Nothing from Kiva. Not even a prayer. 'Walking,' Elya goes on, 'without complaints, prayers, blessings, daredevil tricks, or childish tantrums. Do we see eye to eye?'

They glare at him.

'All in favour, hands up.'

No response.

'Can I see a show of hands?'

'We're not in favour,' says Ziv.

'Really? What about the admirable hours we were going to spend together on the road to Lublin?'

The cousins exchange a secret look.

'I am reproved,' Ziv says, hanging his head. 'As is Kiva.'

Kiva nods.

'Do you mean it?'

'Of course.'

'Good.' Elya is pleased they have reached a consensus. He has stated his case forthrightly as the Uncle would have done and they have understood. Anything can be turned around, he thinks. 'To Lublin!' he cries, leading the way, while behind his back, Ziv pretends to retch up last night's dinner, amusing Kiva.

And so they set off. Kiva, whose father mills the finest grain, whose uncle is the Uncle, whose mother's cousin is a Sobelmann whose family own the best hotel in Mezritsh, sneezes. 'Don't sneeze on me,' says Ziv, who thinks he's on a sightseeing tour, with his foxlike face, his pointed ears, his thumps, pinches, headlocks. And then there is Elya with his dreams of the future, and a future that will be nothing like his dreams.

Descending into a low valley on the third day it grows warmer again, then very warm as the landscape changes to flat fields with few trees. The well-made road shimmers in the sunlight. 'Who made this road?' Elya wonders aloud. 'Adoshem,' says Kiva, but without conviction. He's forgotten his walking stick, if he ever had a walking stick. How can he walk without it? He wants to go back. Go back? Hasn't he heard what Elya's said? They are only going forward now. 'I'll cut you another,' Elya offers. But Kiva doesn't want another. He wants that one. 'It's your fault,' he tells Elya. 'Talking and talking. Talking so much I had to put it down.'

They're all hungry and thirsty. But there is nothing left to eat or drink. They will have to stop soon and purchase supplies. Head thrust forward, map out, Elya aims for the Village of Lakes. Again. Or some other village. Any other village.

'Lublin or die!' he cries.

They pass cultivated fields, haycocks, men at work with scythes in the cloudy heat. Sheaves of cut grain arranged in stooks alarm Kiva when he first sees them, resembling prickly, yellow Cossacks coming over the crest of a hill. There's an irritation of pollen in his nose. Hay asthma, as it is called. Although his cheeks are still rosy from his mother's prune pastries, it won't be long. Pale skin is coming, dilated pupils, bloodstained lips. His prayer books with their wafer-thin pages are still trim and dry and he's vowed to study every day. But by this, the third day, he's too tired. Also they've run out of pure flask water and he cannot wash before prayers as is required. Elya has promised water, first village they come to, and Kiva will do double tomorrow. He's meant to be counting the days, so he'll know when it's the Sabbath, but Kiva has lost track already. On the Sabbath he's obliged to walk slowly if at all; eat three meals; drink raisin wine; wear Sabbath slippers; pray. The Sabbath is not for shouting or running, buying or selling, *vitzing* or *shvitzing*, for thinking impure thoughts, for quarrelling, denouncing, or lusting after neighbours; for carrying anything in your pockets, if you have pockets, or things to carry; or for turning on the gas, if you have gas, to cook a meal. All you can do on the Sabbath is sit around like *drek* on a piece of wood. Marvellous, if you're a weary brushworker, tanner, or shoemaker. No fleshing, drenching, degreasing, bating, stretching, scalding or scudding on the Sabbath. No pounding dung into animal skins. No combing, sorting, cutting, stitching, hammering or spitting nails. In short, all labour ceases for a day. On the Sabbath even demons rest, as do the wicked in Gehenna.

It's also perilously close to the Jewish New Year which will start at sundown on the eighth of Tishri. Ten days later comes the Holy Day of Atonement. Leading up to this solemn day, Jews are supposed to begin a process of self-examination and repentance. In Mezritsh, and other Jewish towns and villages, a ram's horn is blown each morning in the months of Av and Elul, producing a loud, eerie sound meant to awaken Jews from their slumber and alert them: Adoshem with his scythe is coming, reaping and threshing.

'Slow down,' Kiva calls ahead. Another sneeze is imminent. A big one. He wipes his nose on his coat, leaving a long iridescent trail down one sleeve.

Elya cannot bear it. 'Won't you be too warm in that coat?' he enquires.

'The one who suffers most from the heat,' says Kiva, 'is not the one in the heaviest clothes. It's the one with nothing else to think about but his own comfort.'

This is rich coming from Kiva.

At last, he takes it off. Black in colour but lined with silk in a lighter hue, he folds it carefully and hangs it over one arm.

'Can I try it on now?' asks Elya.

Kiva looks doubtful.

'Have you ever worn such a coat?'

'No. But I'd like to. Perhaps I can carry it for you.' Elya reaches out, but Kiva steps away. Then Ziv must get involved.

'What's all this? Fighting over a coat?'

'We're not fighting.'

'No cloth is so fine, moths can't eat it,' Ziv says. Then he looks around. 'Where is this coat?' he asks. 'I don't see any coat.'

'Get your eyes tested.'

'Point to Kiva's coat then,' Ziv stirs the air like a blind man reaching out for something he cannot see, and Elya motions wearily towards one sleeve. What game is this?

'Is a sleeve a coat?' asks Ziv.

'No, of course not.'

'How about a collar?'

'No, a collar is not a coat.'

'Is a hem a coat? A button? An armhole? No, none of the parts of a coat are a coat. Then where's the coat? If we take away all the parts of a coat that are not the coat, the collar, the sleeves, the hem, the buttons, the armholes – the coat disappears.'

'The coat is the collection of its parts,' says Elya.

'If each part is not the coat, how can the collection of parts be the coat?'

'Shut up Ziv.'

'So there is no coat? Am I not holding a coat? *Meyn* coat!' Kiva cries, prepared to believe anything, while Ziv will do anything, say anything, to make mischief.

'There's an absence of coat,' explains Ziv, who is thinking about abandoning all possessions. 'What you thought was there is not there. Not in the way you thought it was.'

Other things that have disappeared, or are disappearing, include: Elya's patience; his future; his shovel; Lublin, increasingly; and the Village of Lakes. Where the fuck is it?

At least they're going in the right direction. He can tell from the sun. But the road is empty. Nothing moving but Elya, Ziv and Kiva. No carriages or horses. No other travellers. Where are all the prosperous merchants who make their rounds from village to village buying whatever produce is in season and selling it on for a profit? Or the thriving pedlars of notions, buttons and combs so prized by villagers and peasants alike? There's only empty road. Why's such a fine wide road so empty?

Ziv hoped to see fast carriages. Not low, open droshkies such as farmers and tradesmen drive, but light two-wheelers. Or high steel-sprung britzkas with retractable roofs like he wants for himself one day, never mind he doesn't believe in private ownership. He'll get in his carriage. Burn up the highway. Straight up the Warsaw Highway in the fast lane. Stay at the best, most expensive lodgings. Check in. Have a wash. Have a schnapps. Have a chat. Have a *shtup* with his *grosser putz*.

A coarse peasant wagon filled with sheep eventually passes; then an old man leading a cow, a child following behind, prodding the creature's hindquarters with a twig; and a two-wheeled cart drawn by farmworkers.

'How far to Lublin?' Elya tries to ask in his *gehakter* Polish. But the farmworkers don't answer.

'They're too tired even to speak,' Ziv opines. Staring after them, he complains about the Tsar again. His counter-reforms in the countryside are reducing the peasants to serfdom once more. 'Every peasant,' Ziv asserts, 'should have the right to support himself and his family on the basis of his own labour.'

'Lift up your feet, or you'll trip,' Elya berates him. 'You're toe-walking again,' he berates Kiva.

'You told us already,' Kiva huffs.

'Yeah,' huffs Ziv.

Then sure enough, Ziv stumbles and falls, bruising his knee and cracking the mirror he carries in his pocket. How will he study his smouldering eyes, big white teeth and shapely mouth now?

'You pushed me, egg-face, chicken-boy,' he cries at Elya. 'I'm not walking any further with him.' Ziv sits down by the side of the road scowling. 'That was my mother's mirror,' he lies.

'I'll be your mirror,' Kiva says.

Ziv thinks he's got a piece of glass in his eye and requires Kiva to have a look. A good look.

'I'm sorry,' Elya tells him. 'I'll buy you a new one, a better one, in Lublin.' He'd say anything to get Ziv moving again. He stretches out a hand and hauls him up. 'I promise.'

'A tall mirror in which I can see my whole body, head to toe.'

'And how will we carry it home?'

'That's your problem.'

Elya would like to hold a mirror up to Ziv's behaviour, but restrains himself.

'What about a mirror-cabinet?' Ziv is thinking of the structures that appeared only recently in the marketplace in Mezritsh. For half a kopek you could enter and see yourself front, sides, and back.

When a goatherd and a flock of goats cross the road, Kiva averts his eyes and holds his nose. Demons live in goats, dropping *bupkes* from their hindquarters. Where once he saw only evidence of Adoshem's wonders, and even the dust was holy, Kiva now sees mostly demons. He wishes he were at morning prayers in a shul inhaling Torah instead of goat turds. Or travelling, if he must, first class in a wagon with a griddle car behind on which kosher meats were cooked for hungry passengers. Ziv must be wishing he were elsewhere too, back among the noble brush and bristleworkers, cracking nuts, spitting shells, playing cards and bad-mouthing the bosses. Anywhere but here. 'You said this would be a holiday,' he complains.

'Like a holiday,' says Elya. 'Wait until we get to Lublin. Lublin potatoes, Lublin women.'

Elya has never eaten a Lublin potato, or seen a Lublin woman, but he's sure both must be large and beautiful. 'You'll thank me one day,' he promises, 'when we're rich and powerful merchants.' But he's shaken by their attitude. They'd turn around for home, if he let them. So, he speaks his mind again. 'May there be no ill will,' he says, 'but in my humble opinion, it has come to my attention . . .'

'Can you make it short,' says Ziv, 'this time?'

'You could both be doing better, walking faster and with more purpose. Do you want to spend the rest of your lives yearning for the men you might have been?'

Both shrug, exchanging glances.

'Are you renouncing your oath?' Elya stares at them in disbelief. 'Your promise to the Uncle to journey swiftly to Lublin for the purpose of selling brushes?'

Despite his low opinion of their intentions, Elya is truly astonished.

'Yes.'

'Yes what?'

'I'm abnegating,' says Ziv.

'You too?'

'I wouldn't say abnegating,' says Kiva. 'I'm considering my options.'

'But we're so close. Lublin's right over there.' Elya points vaguely towards the horizon. 'It's, well, incipient.'

'What the *shtup* does that mean?'

'It's arising.'

'Huh?'

'In the process of becoming.'

'You lost me.'

Why don't they understand? Perhaps Elya is saying it wrong. Incipient? He hates the word. Why doesn't he just say what he means? 'The causes are in place,' he tries again. 'It's only a matter of time. The interval between here and Lublin is getting shorter day by day, hour by hour, minute by minute. You can't give up now.' Elya actually shakes a finger at them. 'It's the wish-fulfilling path.'

'Whose wish, chicken-head?'

'But ... but ... we have a job to do. We're supposed to be turning our dreams into reality.'

'Your dreams.'

'Well, what are your dreams?'

Kiva and Ziv look at each other.

Apparently Ziv would like to be a nightwatchman and chase intruders with a stick. He wouldn't mind soldiering either.

(He would.)

'In the Tsar's Army?' Elya can't believe his ears.

'In the Army of the Brotherhood of Anarchists.'

Ziv also dreams of taking a job in the bristle factory in order to sabotage the works. Secretly he'd like to be a Cossack too, straddling a pair of galloping horses while firing a pistol.

'Not a merchant, then.'

And Kiva?

Kiva thinks ambition might be a sin. He has no ambition other than to study Torah and praise Adoshem, but fears he is losing the will on the road to Lublin.

Elya looks from one to the other with a stunned expression on his face.

'You asked, Mister Bristle,' Ziv says.

'Don't call me that.'

'What? Mister Bristle?'

'Why do you continually obstruct me?'

'Me? It's you. You've changed. The old Elya would have gone back for Kiva's stick. He loved that stick.'

'But we're almost there.'

'Are we really that close?' Kiva sneezes.

'Of course,' says Elya.

'Then we might as well keep going.'

'Ziv?'

'Yeah, all right,' Ziv huffs. 'But I'm not walking any faster, or with purpose.'

XII

The road is long and featureless. Their water flask is empty. Where's the Village of Lakes? Or any village with a standpipe or well?

They begin to get thirsty, then very thirsty. 'Try to ignore it,' says Elya. 'Thirst only for Lublin.' The splash and sprinkle of Lublin's great fountains driving him on. 'What's a little thirst?' he says.

'Piss off.' Ziv turns their water flask upside down and shakes it over his mouth.

'This is the new order of the day. Do not think about drinking. Think of something else.'

Ziv and Kiva look at Elya with contempt.

'Think of the adventure.'

Almost 12,000 feet above sea level in the Himalayas, the city of Lhasa in Tibet, recently invaded by the adventurous British Indian Armed Forces, is found to contain many sacred Buddhist temples, monasteries and palaces. But Ziv's confused. Bundists don't have temples, sacred or otherwise. They meet in people's front rooms that are also their kitchens, in garrets that are also their bedrooms, in shops that are also living quarters, up steep flights of stairs and down dim hallways.

Not Bundists, Ziv. Buddhists.

'What are you going to do when we reach the great city of Lublin?' Elya asks, which might as well be in Tibet at the rate they're going.

'What makes you think we'll ever get there?' says Kiva, sounding like Ziv.

'Let's sit down,' whines Ziv, sounding like Kiva. 'I'm tired and my feet are combusting.'

Elya glares at Ziv's flimsy machine-made shoes. Sightseeing shoes. Shoe Wolf shoes from the busy shop of his father's old rival. Cheap, shoddy and prone to split.

While he waits for Ziv to get up, Elya helplessly recalls his father's stall. He's nothing more than a lad of ten. His father, Usher, is teaching him to mend a shoe. Usher's skilled with his hands, despite missing his right index finger up to the second joint. 'One day, this'll all be yours,' he promises. And young Elya flinches. He drops a tack, picks it up, places it just so. But when he tries to bring the hammer down, Elya misses.

Nimble-fingered he isn't.

'If you look at a hammer long enough, it becomes almost beautiful, no?' Usher is waiting for Elya to take to shoemaking like a bird to the air.

Don't hold your breath Usher.

Ziv's only sock is slipping down below his heel, the skin at the back of both feet rubbed raw. If only he had a plaster, but adhesive bandages will not be invented for years.

'Do you have a hole in your shoe?' Elya asks.

'Not yet.'

'Then how do you get your foot in?'

Pathetic.

Tightly folding his hurt feelings into halves, quarters, eighths, sixteenths, like the tarpaulin he carries, Elya will not open his mouth again.

It's so hot, the road is cracking, oozing tar. Straining under the weight of his overpacked backpack, Kiva, usually white as *shtetl* cheese, is burning red all over as if skinned by Mister Bristle. He takes his large felt hat from his backpack. It's been folded and is creased, possibly ruined, but will keep the sun off his face. Meanwhile Elya, also *shvitzing*, vows never to complain about the cold again. The light is so strong he can barely keep his eyes open. Both hands shading his brow, he wishes for a pair of tinted glasses.

Those who wear tinted glasses are frequently shunned as degenerates in Mezritsh, sensitivity to light being one symptom of the French disease, called the Russian disease in Poland, and the Polish disease in Russia. It'll be years before the use of sunglasses becomes widespread and stigma-free.

In the fields beyond, men and women, bent double, are harvesting. 'Exploited peasants toiling,' Ziv remarks. The peasants shout, waving pitchforks, potato shovels and other farm tools. 'Go home!' they cry.

Possessed by the idea that he'll meet either his father or King Solomon's worm, Ziv forces himself to press on. Presently the road becomes busier. First they pass a man walking in the opposite direction, carrying a brazier on his shoulder. Could this be Ziv's father? No, it cannot. It's a woman disguised as a man. Many women, travelling on their own, travel this way.

'Are we near Lublin?' Elya asks.

'Where?' she says.

'The great city of Lublin.'

'About 150 kilometres,' she says. 'Or more.'

This is of course impossible. Mezritsh is only 102 kilometres from Lublin. And they've been on the road for days.

Never ask a woman directions.

'Women,' Elya rolls his eyes.

Next, they pass a knife- and scissor-grinder carrying his stone wheel on his shoulder. Next, a line of penitents with stones in their shoes, followed closely by invalids, some limping, others pushed in bed carriages. All are searching for a miracle rabbi.

'It's too hot to walk,' whines Kiva, and Elya almost agrees.

In 1902, the first electrical air conditioner is invented. The basic concept is said to have been understood in ancient Egypt, where reeds moistened with trickling water were hung over windows and doors.

Up ahead, another rounded bale of hay arouses Kiva from his torpor. He shrinks back, hiding in Ziv's shadow, and must be led along. Bundles of grain, smelling sickly sweet, dry in the sun. Men with scythes cutting close to the ground are followed by women who gather up the grain and tie it in bundles, followed by stubble-feeding geese. To Elya, every dry field is beginning to look familiar. The peasants also look familiar. Even the geese look familiar. Have they passed this way before? Or is it just the monotony of the road?

Still no Village of Lakes. Or signposts for Lublin.

After walking all morning, these three Jewish boys, with their Jewish faces and Jewish clothes, find themselves unexpectedly approaching a town. In the distance, a crude wooden church with an onion-shaped dome. Russian Town!

Elya, bewildered, studies his map. How have they ended up here? They can go back, retrace their steps, or take a risk and journey on through the town. Going back will mean they've wasted the whole morning. 'Onward,' he cries with such conviction the others must follow, but they do so timidly, even Ziv. The road they are travelling goes right through the town, past low houses with low doors, wooden roofs, tin roofs and straw roofs. Russian houses, Russian roofs, Russian air (don't inhale), Russian trees, and Russian mud that has dried into Russian dust. Walking their Jewish walks, they don't even stop to enquire if there's a standpipe in the town, although they are very, very thirsty.

A big Russian dog lies in the sun, its muzzle in its paws. When it sees them, it gets to its feet and barks. Big Russian faces peer out of small Russian windows. Then something sails over their heads and lands with a great thud at their feet.

A cobblestone.

'Hurry lads. Stay close. Don't look,' says Elya.

They have bribe money pinned to the inside of Kiva's *untervesh*. Will they need to use it? Kiva feels for it just in case. But in the end, it's not necessary. Elya has made the right decision. Or so they think. They have almost reached the edge of the town, when they are stopped by two officials in ill-fitting uniforms, blocking the road. Are they army? Police?

No. Border guards.

'Do you have papers? Permission to travel? Trade permits?' one asks.

Elya looks blankly at them.

'We've done nothing wrong,' says Ziv.

'Then you've nothing to fear.' The Russian leans close and Elya can smell vodka and dogs on his breath.

Tied together with a length of clothesline, they're led down the road to a crude hut, temporary headquarters of the Provincial Chamber of Trade and Commerce, so-called. There's one wooden desk, two chairs, and a picture of the Tsar on the wall.

Elya, Kiva and Ziv are untied, then made to stand shoulder to shoulder while the bigger of the two border guards pokes their bedrolls and backpacks. 'Sleeping in fields is against the law for Jews,' he says. The smaller Russian, who's not that small, agrees. Both have short, thick Russian noses and little eyes. Neither likes the look on Ziv's face, or the way he stands. Ziv gives them a contemptuous smile. And Elya thinks, we're dead. He looks down at his feet, studying his shoes, Kiva's shoes, Ziv's shoes, the Russians' short, thick boots, anywhere but at their scowling faces.

'What's this?' The big Russian lifts their precious brush case. He opens it and sneers. 'You'll never sell these.' He picks up a brush, passing it from hand to hand scornfully. 'Kuznetsevchev, look at this.'

But Kuznetsevchev is looking at Kiva, grabbing the sleeve of the fine coat he carries. 'Feel that fabric,' he remarks like one who knows its value. 'Where does a Jew pedlar get such a coat? Stolen?' He leers at Kiva who's already handing over his precious coat. 'And the hat.' The Russian indicates the traditional black fedora Kiva's wearing made of fine wool felt. Kuznetsevchev puts it on. 'You look like a Jew,' Egorushkinski laughs. In response, Kuznetsevchev tilts the hat at a rakish angle. More laughter. Then Egorushkinski puts it on. Then Kuznetsevchev grabs it back. The coat is greatly admired and they both try it on as well, warning each other to be careful as it will fetch an excellent price.

'What about you?' Egorushkinski turns to Elya. 'Are you loyal to the Tsar?' Pinching Elya by one ear, the Russian drags him to the wall where a picture of His Imperial Majesty the Supreme Autocrat hangs, hair neatly parted to the left, pointed moustache, pug nose.

'I greatly admire the Tsar,' says Elya in his *gehakter* Russian. Pale and stammering, he places his hand on his heart. 'He is a fine and true leader.'

'Kneel, brush pedlar,' Egorushkinski tells him and Elya immediately falls to his knees.

Standing on a chair, Kuznetsevchev lifts down the portrait of Tsar Nicholas II, bringer of pogroms, and hands it to Egorushkinski, who thrusts it in Elya's face. Elya kisses the image, tasting dust.

'The Tsar has golden blood,' Elya says.

'Golden blood, eh?' The Russians nod.

'OK. You can go,' Kuznetsevchev says abruptly, waving the lads away like wagon flies.

They pick up their backpacks, bedrolls and brush case.

'Not you,' Egorushkinski points to Ziv. 'Are you also loyal to the Tsar?'

In response Ziv makes a sound low in his throat.

Oh God, thinks Elya, he's going to spit.

'He's simple-minded.' Kiva cuts in front of Ziv. 'We're looking after him.'

'Is that so?' The Russians regard Ziv enthusiastically.

'You cannot hold me. I know my rights,' says Ziv in his excellent Russian.

Not so simple-minded after all.

Egorushkinski leans forward and punches him in the face.

After a stunned silence, Ziv begins to cry, shamefully, which makes the Russians laugh out loud.

'Go before we change our mind,' Kuznetsevchev says to Elya and Kiva. 'He stays.'

Elya is already edging to the door, his full money belt as yet undiscovered. If he can only get away before they notice. But Kiva remains. He offers the Russians the bribe money he secretly carries in exchange for Ziv.

And they take it.

All of it.

The lads run with their packs on their backs, bedrolls and brush case bobbing, putting as much distance as they can between themselves and Russian Town. Normally Kiva is not allowed to run. Running could bring on a fit. But running is required sometimes, no?

'Where's your pocket watch?' Elya pants, when they finally stop to rest, still trembling like little birds.

'Well hidden,' Kiva coughs and splutters, removing it from his underwear.

'They took your coat!' Elya is outraged.

'He gave it to them!' Ziv is also outraged.

It wasn't a coat. It was only the appearance of a coat, as Ziv has already explained. No coat was taken, as no coat existed. So, why's Ziv outraged? He's outraged by the manner in which it was given away. Despite his injuries, a thick lip and a bloody nose, he is not angry at the Russians; he's angry at his so-called friends.

'I lost my head,' Elya admits, 'but Kiva was brave.'

'He was stupid. You panicked, Kiva,' says Ziv. 'You and Elya. They were nothing but fakers. I don't even think they were Russians. Border guards? My eye. Everything was phoney. The uniforms were phoney, the hut was phoney.'

'The interrogation room?'

'The so-called interrogation room. That painting on the wall? That wasn't even the Tsar. He doesn't have a pug nose.'

'He does.'

'They had no right to hold us. There were three of us and only two of them.'

'Did you see the size of them?'

'Let's go back and sort them out. Who's with me?'

Elya and Kiva look at him like he's crazy.

'I hate the Tsar,' Ziv mutters. 'You kissed him. Traitor.'

'What about his reforms?' Elya knows a thing or two about Russian politics.

'What, are you an Octobrist? The October Manifesto was rubbish. Promising political reform, elections, civil liberties. All lies.'

'He created a parliament.'

'Then he dissolved it. Twice!' Ziv catches Elya in a headlock and wrestles him to the ground. 'You're a Tsarist.'

'I'm not.'

How can a Jew be a Tsarist? And before he can stop himself, Elya is telling a *vitz*. One of his best.

'*Two Jews decide to kill the Tsar. They sneak into the Alexandra Palace and hide behind the door to his bedroom. Hour after hour they wait with beating hearts. But he doesn't arrive. Finally one turns to the other. "I hope nothing's happened to him, God forbid."*'

Not even a smile from his blank-faced, stony-faced, wooden-faced friends.

'What's that supposed to mean?' Kiva is puzzled.

'It means he's a Tsarist,' says Ziv.

'It's a joke,' says Elya.

'Huh?'

Ziv laughs at danger, speeding carriages, *shlongs*, *putzes*, *shmucks*, *drek* and anything that reeks of *drek*, fat people, frightened people, people falling or pushed down stairs, into holes, trenches, ravines, gullies. The only thing Ziv doesn't laugh at is Elya's jokes. Except once. Once he laughed. Maybe twice. It's not Ziv's fault. It's a cruel, indifferent time and suffering is often considered funny. In Coney Island, America, Topsy the elephant is electrocuted in 1903 for amusement in front of a small crowd of invited guests. Filmed, to be viewed in coin-operated kinetoscopes across America, the footage still exists and can be watched electronically today. But who would want to see such a thing?

Would you?

Elya ponders his cowardly behaviour as they walk on. Back in Russian Town, he was prepared to abandon Ziv to save his own skin and his money belt. Ziv is becoming more than irritating, but still. Are those the actions of a leader? As he walks, he thinks of all the things he should have done. Even ending up in Russian Town was his fault, distracted when he should have been paying attention to his map. He's disappointed with himself and full of doubts. Maybe his friends are right and they should turn around for home before something even worse happens. As is, they've had a lucky escape. Why struggle against great odds? He hangs his head. Nothing has gone right. He's a hopeless leader. Like the Tsar, *may his head be full of lice and his arms too short to scratch.*

Tonight, Elya will sit down with the map and find the quickest route home; for now they must continue on. Turning back now would mean Russian Town again. There are no other roads. Only this road. Could they trespass across cultivated fields? With a shudder, Elya considers the local *Kapitans* and labouring peasants. Continue on, he decides, then look for another way home tonight. Thinking of home, his mother's chickens come unbidden to mind, running and flapping, but never taking off.

'Why did the prickly plant cross the road?'

Ziv doesn't know. 'Why?'

'It was attached to a chicken.'

Miserable faces all round.

The chicken is a flightless bird adapted to living on the ground; a heavy bird with small wings. Other *shtetl* birds are as vulnerable. Whistling, preening, nest-building, pecking themselves and each other, rolling in mud, noshing on bird cherries, they are caught in the whirlwind of hand-cranked machinery; trapped under falling doors; packed tightly into small suitcases; locked in cupboards; roofed in pastry, lured inside ovens and baked into pies.

Walking slightly ahead of his friends, but without his former pace or determination, miserable with failure and remorse, Elya hears something behind them and stops, heart hammering. The others hear it too. A harsh sound in the distance like a kitchen knife sharpened on a stone.

'Hide!' Elya shouts as he feels the ground begin to shake and they all dive into the bushes at the side of the road. Just then, a flash of metal glinting in the sunlight, a rush of air, a roar of lions, a honking of geese, and a motor car comes around the bend.

Elya stands and stares after it. 'Did you see that? Did you?' A sharp bitter smell, like kerosene, but not. And a hot, oily cloud of smoke. It all happens so quickly Elya is unable to determine if it's a Benz, a Daimler or a Maybach. He's so excited he jumps up and down on the spot. He's going to have a vehicle with a four-stroke internal combustion engine just like that some day. But how, if he doesn't make his mark as a seller of brushes? All at once he's reminded of his excellent purpose. Even poor men like Elya can rise into money if they have a worthy goal to which they are committed, and for which they are willing to endure danger and great hardship, risking even their own lives, and the lives of their friends. Elya can exact a profit from any situation. He can sell shadows, smoke, snow. He'll spin deals wherever he goes. He doesn't need a comfortable bed or a soft pillow. He doesn't need a hot meal. He'd be happy eating berries from a thorny bush. Contemplating this, he feels newly invigorated. Go home? Now? Never! Setbacks will only make him stronger. He stiffens his shoulders, prepared to neither eat, nor drink, nor sleep until Lublin.

What does a Russian bride get from her husband on her wedding day that's long and hard?' a restored Elya asks his friends.

'A new last name!'

It's the kind of joke Ziv might have told and it's a success. They all laugh together.

'What do you call a beautiful girl in Russian Town?'

Elya is going for two in a row.

'A tourist.'

He should have stopped while he was ahead.

XIII

By mid-afternoon the light is blinding. They stumble past bushes wilting in the sun, a parched farm road, and a peasant cart filled with newly harvested beets already covered in dust. 'Hup, hup,' the peasant says to his old horse. Everyone is more than thirsty. Ziv complains of muscle cramps; his piss is brown and nothing more than a dribble. He used to piss like a bull, he brags. Now he's pissing dust.

Kiva needs a drink or a cucumber or he'll die. '*Wasser*,' he sobs without tears. He is so dehydrated no tears will come. Elya promises a standpipe in the next village. His own tongue is as dry as an empty barrel, a burned potato, the goodbye kiss he gave Libka. He can hear the sound of rushing water, dripping water, water being poured from a pitcher, but it must be his ears. 'When we find a well, and we will find one, it'll be like you've never drunk anything as sweet. And wait until you taste Lublin water. Lublin!' he shouts.

'Go to hell,' Ziv tells him.

'Yeah,' says Kiva.

Otherwise they don't speak, their words drying up on their swollen tongues. According to Kiva, they only have a limited number of words anyway given to them by Adoshem. When all their allotted words have been spoken, they will die. But how many do they have? This is a mystery. No one knows the number of words at their disposal. Or how many times they can repeat them. 'I think you've reached your limit,' Ziv tells Elya, when he next attempts to spur them on.

They walk single file without speaking, until they encounter a band of grim-faced women, the abandoned wives one hears so much about these days, looking in one small village after another for their errant husbands. Forbidden by Jewish law to remarry or have any relationship with men, these women, called the *aguna* or chained women, have taken to the road together. They cannot free themselves from marriage without their husband's consent, or a writ signed by one hundred rabbis. Where are they going to find one hundred rabbis? Or their errant husbands? They stream forward at a breathless pace, even in this heat, so great is their intention. Why can't Kiva and Ziv walk as fast? Some are still young and attractive. Many wear 'modesty shoes', from the last century, that button over the ankle. They all want to tell Ziv their stories. He looks at them with interest and pity. For all his love of rebellion and new ideas, it never occurs to Ziv to question the institution of marriage, but he feels sorry for these women all the same. Ziv's own mother, abandoned by his father long ago, could have been one of them.

'They have water for sale,' he tells Elya.

Elya disapproves, but they are very thirsty. 'OK,' Elya hands him a coin. 'Give them a kopek.'

'They want five kopeks.'

'Five kopeks!'

'A sip.'

'That's preposterous! Nothing doing!'

But as Elya turns to walk away, Ziv makes a grab for the purse he wears around his waist. They wrestle for it. 'This is all your fault,' cries Ziv, knocking Elya to the ground. 'My fault?' Elya jumps up. 'I tried to stop you and Kiva. But you wouldn't listen. You both drank heedlessly.'

'We did not. It was you. Your *farkakta* flask leaked.'

'You want to spend all our money on sips of water?' Elya gasps. 'Well I say no, as long as I'm purse.'

'Who made you purse? I'll be purse. And leader.'

'You? Never! You ought to be glad it's me. While I'm purse we won't run out of money. And that's a promise!'

'What good is money when you're dead?'

'Dead?'

'From thirst.'

The *aguna* quickly overtake them. Soon they're only a blur on the horizon while silent, thirsty and dazed, Elya and his so-called friends walk on, shading their eyes, opening their shirts, rolling up their sleeves. Anyone else would have stopped and found a shady place to rest, but Elya sets a hasty pace, promising water around the next bend, or the one after that. The quicker they walk, the sooner they'll find a standpipe or a well. And sure enough, in the distance, Elya sees a bright body of silvery water shimmering in the sun. He runs blindly towards it. But when he reaches the spot, he finds nothing there. Looking ahead there are more shimmering lakes which are only tricks of light.

'Gimme that map,' says Ziv, 'you'll get us lost again.'

'We weren't lost. We're following in the footsteps of other venerable merchants. How could we be lost?'

'Then why did we end up in Russian Town, eh? And where's the *farkakta* Village of Lakes?' Ziv makes a grab for Elya's map.

'We should have taken a coach,' Kiva gripes. 'You're as stingy as my uncle. We could have been there by now.'

The coach from Mezritsh to Lublin is only fourteen hours including rest stops, but Uncle deemed it too expensive.

'How do you think he got to be the Uncle?' says Elya. 'While I am leader, we walk!'

'You had your chance,' says Ziv.

'Yeah,' says Kiva.

'You put us in danger. You don't let us have any fun,' says Ziv.

'Prune Town,' says Kiva.

'Someone has to take the hard decisions,' says Elya. 'If I left it to you we'd never have come.'

'We never should have come!'

'But we're here.'

'Starving, thirsty, hot.'

'You can't blame me for the weather.'

'It was your idea to come in August. We should have waited.'

'Waited for what? The grabbers who patrol the roads in autumn?'

Elya's right. They look around shamefaced. Many young men have already been taken by these unscrupulous bounty hunters, called *Khappers*, and drafted into the Russian army. The forced conscription of Jewish men and boys between the ages of thirteen and thirty is the law, as it has been for generations.

Married men are still exempt and hasty weddings are arranged. Some boys drink black coffee to speed up their heart rates and appear unfit, or rouge their teeth to resemble a consumptive spitting blood, or run to America, or run south, out of Poland, to a land beyond Galicia. Every morning *shtetl* boys are missing. *Khappers* are even known to burst into houses, which is how poor Mordy Peepzeit was taken. Any boy can be taken. One minute a boy is here, next minute, *a zay gezunt, unt a gute nacht.*

The wealthy can bribe Russian officials and buy back a Jewish child. But if they don't have money, families must take drastic measures. So that the lad cannot fire a gun and is therefore exempt, the cutting off of the right index finger up to the second joint has always been a common practice.

Some lads like Elya's brother Fishel hang about actually hoping to be caught. Fishel wants a gun to fire. He wants to march eight abreast through villages and towns with his sword unsheathed. He wants the close-fitting white jacket and peaked white cap of a Russian soldier, which unfortunately makes them conspicuous in the field, resulting in many casualties in a recent war with Japan.

I'm a good leader, Elya thinks, no matter what Ziv says. Steady, earnest, responsible, thrifty, prudent. Elya vows to protect them, hand on heart. So he's made a few mistakes. So what? Elya's role as leader is as indisputable as the excellent road map he carries, drawn by the admirable company of Mezritsher merchants. 'We continue as we were,' he says. Feeling his voice grow stronger, firmer, louder, he orders his friends to walk on. And they do, Kiva whining, Ziv grumbling, his shoes giving way at every step. 'If we don't reach Lublin by tomorrow, we'll turn back,' Elya promises. It won't be the first promise he has broken, nor the last. Kiva makes a prayer face and asks Adoshem to bless Elya's map.

'Excuse me,' he says to Adoshem, 'I'm going to sneeze.'

Only soft boys sneeze, thinks Elya, growing as callous as Ziv.

Crouched behind his heavy backpack, Kiva sneezes six times in a row. That's how soft he is. Poor Kiva.

'He needs a rest,' says Ziv, growing soft as Kiva. 'How about lunch?' And before Elya can protest, Ziv hops over a blistered fence beside a sign that reads: NIE WCHODZIC.

Elya and Kiva follow warily, calling Ziv to come back. Now! Ignoring them, Ziv enters a field of smooth, low grass. This is more like it. 'Watch me.' He does handstands and cartwheels. Meanwhile in the distance, a large black bull lowers his head and stomps the ground.

No one is speaking to Ziv when they regain the road, hearts pounding, legs shaking. When they stop for lunch at last, it's on a dry slope, a place chosen by Elya, surrounded by stinging fronds, snake leaves, unidentified bracken and burdock.

'You call this grass?' Ziv complains. 'My place was better.'

Coming to rest in the thin shade of a thorn bush, Elya unpacks his tarp and would put out food, if they had any food. Absent-mindedly, Kiva chews the edge of his prayer book which tastes a bit like a bad prune. Imitating Kiva, Ziv removes, then chews his shoes. They are disintegrating anyway, the fancy uppers shrivelling in the heat. 'I could murder a potato,' he says, regretting all the comely potatoes he didn't eat. But there are no potatoes. Except for the two in Elya's pocket: one rescued from the long grass where it was thrown by Ziv, the other from the side of the road, also thrown by Ziv. Elya's saving them for an emergency. But what's this if not an emergency? Other things in Elya's pockets include: a silver coin his mother gave him; Libka's prune pit; a sock; a map; dirt; a bird cherry sprig; a tarry indefinable smell; a medium-size hole; and anything that might have fallen through that hole into the dark lining beneath.

Pulling each other's hair, clothes, ears, they fight over the potatoes Elya fishes out. Ziv, who has the biggest appetite, thinks he should have the most. But Elya divides them equally.

'Perhaps the ravens will feed us,' Kiva looks up to the sky, 'as they fed Elijah the Prophet, twice daily from the King's table.'

Harried by the eight hundred and fifty false prophets of Ba'al, according to Kiva, Elijah is searching for the hundred true prophets of legend, who are hiding from the wrath of Ahab under floorboards, behind false doors, between stacks of split wood, or in the clefts of rocks overhanging a forest.

'Shut up Kiva. You wanted a rest, let's just rest,' Elya says.

The ground is furrowed with shallow twisting roots and Ziv shifts, uncomfortable on his haemorrhoids. Even Elya and Kiva who do not have haemorrhoids feel as if they are sitting on burning twigs. If he were to die right now, Kiva tells the others, he wouldn't mind. (He would.) Ziv pummels him, but his heart isn't in it. Maybe later. Eventually he gets to his feet. He has a fat Russian lip and a bruised Russian eye. He traces a worm in the dusty grass with his half-eaten shoe then walks off. Not far from where they are sitting, he finds a tree with parched leaves and begins to climb.

'Come down,' Kiva sneezes, while Ziv, who thinks he's indestructible, climbs higher and higher, disappearing between the branches and shaking the dry leaves.

'Can you see Lublin?' Elya calls up to him.

Finally, but only after Elya and Kiva think they've lost him forever, Ziv descends. 'Look, I can fly!' He jumps from a low branch, lands heavily, and turns his ankle painfully, blaming the tree.

Watching Ziv's antics, Elya recalls how he once wanted to be just like him and shakes his head. He tries to bring to mind Ziv's virtues but can think of none. He remembers Ziv aged ten strutting around the courtyard behind their houses, whistling. '*Kumen do,*' he invites Elya to join the group of boys that crowd around him: the twins, Yossel and Yankel Steckler; Ziv's cousin Akiva Goldfarb, known as Kiva; Pinchus Zilbert; Nistor Kahanovitch; Benesh Bergelson; and Avram Hofshteyn.

Is he serious? Who, me? Elya can't believe it. Fearing a trick, he hesitates. The group of boys are peeking into a cellar window where a *moid* is getting undressed. Ziv, in front, pressing his nose right up against the glass. Elya behind, eyes popping. But she's a dog. 'A *hundt,*' says Ziv, loudly barking, and they all shriek with laughter, Elya included.

'*Farmakhn ir pisherkehs!*' Mrs Tabachnic, no teeth, red face, opens her window, leans out and shakes a fist at them. 'Is that Elya Grynberg with Ziv Nagelbach?' She stares hard at Elya, who is known to be a good boy.

The courtyard is a cobbled, roofless space surrounded by the backs of wooden houses and high stone walls. It's crowded with makeshift sheds and structures belonging to the tenants, barrels, prams, carts, and cages for small animals and birds, and so criss-crossed with clothes lines a running boy could be throttled. In one corner, a fearsome row of outhouses, damp underfoot and always cold, except when fiery with excrement.

Ziv walks along the edge of one wall, sending down a rain of dry mortar. Suddenly losing his balance, he slips and lands with a thud. Is he dead? The boys and girls crowd around him. Eventually he gets up, dazed but smiling. Next thing you know, he's lighting a small rag fire. Everyone cheers.

Another neighbour, Mrs Kosakoff, runs out her back door and tries to hit Ziv with a broom, while her husband stamps on the burning rags. *'May you go on a nice long trip,'* she curses Ziv, *'and die far from home.'*

A Jewish curse is like a terrible prophesy, often enticing the victim with the promise of good fortune, then yanking it away at the last minute and replacing it with misery. Ziv shrugs. Big deal. *'You should find a gold piece on the ground, Mrs Kosakoff, but be so arthritic you can't even bend down to pick it up.'*

The light is bright and cloudy at the same time, which is hard to endure even without a headache. There's a bad smell from a stagnant pond nearby. Ziv and Kiva talk about those who might have come, were invited to come, but were smart enough not to. Like Yossel and Yankel who are at this very moment noshing on poppy seed bread, chickpeas from a paper cone, and schmaltz herring from the food stalls of Mezritsh. 'Drinking water,' cries Ziv, 'tea; bird cherry cordial; getting *shikker* on schnapps; kiss-fighting with the girls on the riverbank.'

'Instead of walking down an endless road *shvitzing*,' adds Kiva.

'It's not endless,' says Elya.

Blackflies, worse than mosquitoes, hover and bite. Ziv sneaks a peek in his ruined mirror, but can only see half his face. Kiva takes out his prayer book, but can only read half a prayer. His head is swimming. He feels first hot then cold and needs to cough or sneeze. Eventually he squeezes out a whole prayer, straining and grunting. Because they have lost the latrine shovel and Kiva is afraid of venturing alone into the woods ever again, the infrequency of his bowel movements, cramped and hard as balls of shot, or small animal droppings, is making him dull and slow. This afternoon, however, something more significant is stirring in his lower abdomen. Leaving the others, he walks as far as he dares into the surrounding woods to do his business. Carefully he picks his way through low scrub. At last he stops, undoes the buttons on his trousers and squats, ready to perform the most secret of functions. Beneath his feet, leaf litter, as unclean as real litter. He stares at a tree, the bark running with beetles. Suddenly there's a sound behind him. When he turns around, he sees them, crouched low, watching.

Cossacks?

No. Ground squirrels!

Abruptly getting up, then running, his trousers slipping, he catches his foot and pitches forward, slamming his shoulder painfully into a tree. As a result, his shoulder will turn black and blue and his bowels will close up again. Maybe forever.

'Crybaby,' Ziv sneers when Kiva returns sobbing and coughing.

'Don't talk to him like that,' says Elya. 'Can't you see he's had a fright? I thought you were his friend.'

'He's a baby. And you're an old man.'

'And you're a bully. Get off my tarp. You can't sit here any more.'

'Unfair,' Ziv complains, but he gets up and walks away, snapping his big teeth. Picking up a fallen branch, he uses it to beat a tree. With a mighty snap, he pulls down a healthy bough, then shakes a young sapling. He eventually finds a stump to sit on. He glares at Elya and Kiva then opens his book and begins to read, while Kiva prays for more potatoes, fewer flies, and a coat for Elya.

'A good one like yours was,' says Elya.

A new batch of insect bites are starting to appear on Kiva's arms, Elya's neck, Ziv's ankles. Soon they will become hard, red and itchy. Kiva compares his to Elya's. 'Mine are worse,' he says.

Burrs of burdock sticking to their clothes, they regain the road. Ziv's ankle is painful and he doesn't think he can walk very far. Above their heads, a tree full of woodcocks. If they'd but known. Elya unfolds his map. Kiva sneezes. Then, as if by a miracle, the Village of Lakes appears around the next bend.

But the Village of Lakes, as it turns out, is actually the Village of Sticks. According to Elya's unmistaken map, the Village of Sticks ought to have been found elsewhere, beyond the Village of Girls, but before the Village of Prayers, none of which have they encountered, in this order or any order. Eh? What gives? And where are all the ordinary towns between Mezritsh and Lublin? Radzyn? Stavaitchi? Vlodva? Lubartov? Skrobow? Serniki? Niemce? Tarow?

The streets piled high with lumber are lined with wooden houses behind wooden fences and wooden shops with wooden roofs. A woman sitting on a bundle of sticks ignores them, then grimaces as they pass.

When they find a standpipe, Ziv puts his head under the spout.

'Nectar!' Elya drinks from his hands. 'I told you,' he crows. 'And it's free.'

Kiva recites a blessing, water dribbling down his chin. It must be a different type of water here, because it tastes fantastic. They fill their flask, drink it down, fill it up again. Drink it down again. Toast each other, gripping shoulders, forearms.

'To the future!'

'The future!'

Ziv throws a punch. Kiva goes down and they both laugh. Then Ziv knuckles Elya, who knuckles him right back.

In a small outdoor market they are able to buy buckwheat groats from a shrewd-faced peasant, but the crisp, salted biscuits, fashioned into ropes and twisted in knots (like Kiva's intestines) are deemed too expensive by Elya, who carefully guards their purse.

'Not even one pretzel to share?'

'Say again?' Elya inclines his head, pretending not to hear.

New shoes are nearly purchased for Ziv, who protests. Rescued from a shoe fire, they're blistered in places. He'd rather have a pair of *valenki* made of felt, or cheap, short-lived bast shoes woven from tree bark like the peasants wear. The Russians call these *lapti*, which is also a derogatory term for those too poor to afford better.

A crude wooden shovel is purchased for Elya. Kiva is bought a sneeze remedy. Ziv gets a newspaper.

EMPEROR WILHELM OF GERMANY TO MEET THE TSAR; BOLSHEVIKS IN TIFLIS; DROUGHT SET TO CONTINUE, WHEN WILL IT RAIN? The headlines are weeks old. Ziv throws the paper away in disgust, longing for a precious current copy of the Bundist *Alarm Clock*, the *Workers' Voice*, the hateful, reactionary *Mezritsher Trytuna* or even the mind-numbing *Mezritsher Wachenblatt* – *may it spontaneously combust.*

Elya picks up the discarded paper, which will come in handy for either fire-starting or *tochus*-wiping. Then Ziv comes up behind him, grabs his ears, holding them tight between his fingers, and twists until Elya cries out.

Leaving the village, they pass a man operating a machine for turning and shaping articles of wood. Beside him, two men, slowly and with much effort, try to cut a stone with a narrow-bladed double saw in a wooden frame, putting Ziv in mind of King Solomon's worm. If he had such a worm, he'd toss it down the back of Elya's shirt right now. Then he'd let it loose on the stone houses of the rich on Lubliner Street in Mezritsh.

Outside the village blacksmith's, they recognise the motor car they encountered earlier. It is parked and empty. Elya rubs his eyes, blinks. He approaches the vehicle open-mouthed. Headlamps! Pneumatic tyres! A five-sided hood with folding hinges! Brass fittings! He can't take it all in. He has the urge to climb into the driver's seat upholstered in leather, but dares not. What if the owner returns? Ziv has no such qualms. He jumps into the high-wheeled vehicle and sits behind the steering mechanism. Turning it this way and that, Ziv tries to feel excited, but it isn't what he really wants.

If they can but hang on, soon everyone will get their heart's desire. Elya will have the opportunity to sell a mountain of paint-brushes, more brushes than there are walls to paint. Ziv will have a wolf's dinner, a beautiful woman, and a fight in an alley half-flooded by an open drain. And Kiva? Kiva will speak with Adoshem who will explain the meaning of life.

That night they camp beside a big mud-coloured lake, shrinking from its banks. They fish with makeshift rods but catch nothing for their dinner except crayfish, which are not kosher fish and cannot be eaten. 'Why don't we swim across?' Ziv asks.

'It's too far,' says Elya.

Kiva agrees. He's not much of a swimmer.

Ziv shrugs. His flimsy machine-made shoes fall from his feet. He peels off his sock, his shirt, trousers, underwear. His bruises have faded and his body is taut and slim. Naked, he imitates Kiva's bird walk, his potato walk, his sneeze walk. 'Kiss *mein geshtorben*!' He bends over and spreads his bottom cheeks in Kiva's face. Then, *pisher* and *knedelach* swinging, he jumps in the lake, while Kiva and Elya watch from the shore where weeds droop and parched willows sag.

'Herr Doktor *is drowning in a river*,' says Elya, and Kiva groans.

'*An excited crowd gathers as he's pulled out. "Give him artificial respiration," someone in the crowd suggests.*

"*Never," cries Herr Doktor's haughty wife. "It's real respiration or nothing!*"'

After Ziv's swim, Elya relents and lets him sit on his tarp again. They're almost friends. Silently they watch night fall. Twilight first, with enough light in the sky to read. Then dusk. At dusk, there will be no more reading. It's the darkest part of twilight, just before the night. Soon, thinks Elya, Lublin dusk.

After dark, Ziv forgets himself and whistles. Oh no. Bad luck. They all laugh from nerves. They don't even wrestle or give each other dead limbs now. Instead they sit morosely in front of the fire they've built, barely speaking.

'Aren't you going to pray?' Ziv asks Kiva.

'Later.'

With his new but inferior shovel, Elya digs a latrine especially for Kiva, Ziv looking on. 'I like the way you dug that,' Ziv comments. 'Now jump in.'

Dinner is *batampta* kasha. 'The best kasha you ever ate,' promises Elya. But when he tries to erect another cooking crane, the handle of his new shovel catches fire. Then the cooking pot must be propped up on rocks and positioned right over the flames instead. Consequently, the pot, and the kasha inside the pot, burn. There is also no salt.

'Is it *geshmak?*'

No. It's burned, dry, tasteless and hard.

'What's kasha without salt?' asks Ziv.

'*Drek.*'

Kiva, chewing and swallowing without tasting, thinks helplessly of his mother's salty kasha, each grain plump as a pillow. Then he smells gunpowder. That's not gunpowder, Kiva, that's burned kasha. Ziv chases him around the campsite and when he catches him, thumps Kiva on the head with his prayer book once, twice, three times. Then Elya does it. What now? A spitting competition? Or a poem? Ziv can recite any number of protest verses of his own dedicated to the workers of the world. 'Let the ruling classes tremble,' he cries.

'Not so loud. Someone might hear,' Kiva looks towards the darkening forest and the empty road beyond, while Ziv recites his latest.

'*Up above the sea's grey flatland, wind is gathering the clouds . . .* '

He is passing off a poem by the revolutionary Russian writer Maxim Gorky as his own. Written in 1901, 'The Song of the Stormy Petrel' is composed in a variation of unrhymed trochaic tetrameter with occasional pyrrhic substitutions.

Huh?

'Is there more? Can we hear the rest?'

'Later,' says Ziv. A new poem is coming and he must write it down now before he forgets. He asks to borrow Elya's pencil, then hesitates. 'What rhymes with parasites?' he enquires.

'Mites.'

'Bites.'

'Tights.' (Not yet invented.)

'Rights, lights, nights, fights.'

Ziv's new poem will be about the glorious mutineers aboard the battleship *Potemkin* who rebel against their officers after being made to eat, at gunpoint, borscht prepared with meat partially infested with maggots and other parasites. 'Parasites' also refers to the industrialists who are getting rich off the backs of the workers. Then, having taken over the vessel, the rebels sail for Odessa flying the red flag.

Ziv would like to be a mutineer one day. Or a saboteur. Does he even know the difference? A mutineer refuses to obey the orders of someone in authority. A saboteur deliberately destroys something. All right, he'll be both.

'Let's see who's got the biggest *putz*,' Ziv says next. He jumps up, unbuttoning his trousers. It's Ziv, naturally. Kiva's a surprising second, and Elya's a disappointing third. Ziv and Kiva stare at Elya's third-rate *putz* until it seems to shrink even further. Soon they are bored again, and Ziv offers to read aloud from the Russian novel he's been devouring.

There is a female character in the story, Ziv tells them, compelled to service men for money to help her starving family.

What does this mean?

'You know, *shtupping.*' Ziv makes a rude gesture and Kiva turns away while Elya thinks helplessly of his own sister Rifka left behind in Mezritsh. Don't contemplate that, he tells himself. She's only twelve and has visions which embarrass the whole family. But he's worried about her all the same. What if Klara's chickens die and there's no egg money coming in? Rifka would have to help out. People say she looks like him. She's half pretty, half not. He tries to imagine her in a slippery dress attempting to attract men. Rifka in the arms of a horse trader, or a herring pickler. A *shlepper* of heavy goods bouncing Rifka on his knee.

He remembers her as a child telling anyone who'll listen about the *farkakta* games she invents. A game about people searching for bread and papers. What bread? What papers? What kind of game is that? People walking with their hands up in the air? Why can't she play normal girls' games like *Ittle-Bittle* with a piece of string? Luckily everyone ignores her.

Back home in Mezritsh, Rifka is most likely doing nothing out of the ordinary, breaking eggs, burning pots, washing behind Zusa's ears, or playing a new game she calls 'Forced Labour', in which Zusa is compelled to do Rifka's sweeping. Or the dying game in which Rifka is *Herr Doktor* and Zusa pretends to die, then Zusa is *Herr Doktor* and Rifka pretends to die. In the end, they're both dead.

At last, all thoughts of Rifka disappear and Elya's back on his tarpaulin with Kiva and Ziv. From the nearby lake comes the sound of wild splashing, after which it's quiet again. Can you die of insect bites? Kiva picks a bite on his elbow until it bleeds. They're all sitting a little distance from each other. The dark is even darker than before. 'Who has the best knapsack?' asks Kiva. Not Ziv. The best shoes? Not Ziv. The best beard? Not Ziv. The best jokes? Not Elya!

Who has the best mosquito bites?

Kiva!

Kiva rolls up his trousers to scratch his leg with one hand, while clawing a bite on his neck with the other. Then the game of best and worst is over. Or is it? 'What's the worst, most shameful thing you've ever done?' asks Ziv.

Mindel, Kiva thinks.

'I'm not telling,' he says.

'Why not?' Ziv throws a punch. Kiva ducks but not quickly enough. It lands on the back of his neck. Elya just watches. Should he take a swing at Kiva too? Or should he take a swing at Ziv?

'I once ate a whole cake,' Kiva gasps at last.

'I did something much worse. I was the lad who painted DEATH TO THE BOSSES on the marketplace walls,' says Ziv, who did no such thing. He wasn't even there.

'I'm telling,' says Kiva.

'You're dead,' says Ziv.

The beatings Ziv receives from his mother who adores him but frequently loses control, and the beatings he metes out to smaller, weaker boys in the alleys of Mezritsh, are his real secret, untold.

Elya has no secrets and has done nothing to be ashamed of, if he ignores the deathbed promise he made his father.

According to Kiva, all our deeds and thoughts, including secrets, are recorded in the Book of Memory kept by Adoshem, who is everywhere and always watching, like the busybodies of Mezritsh.

Elya wants to discuss their stock and how they will best sell it. But he sees his friends' eyes grow dim whenever he mentions commerce. Nonetheless he continues, proposing a trial run of sales tomorrow in the Village of Fools, an easy target before they reach Lublin. It's on the way. They must be close. Get there early. Hire a trestle in the marketplace. Sell. Sell. Sell.

'Mister Bristle,' Ziv calls Elya again, his voice an elbow-poke. 'Here comes Mister Bristle. Look out, it's Mister Bristle.'

So? Elya decides he doesn't mind the name. Mister Bristle? He quite likes it.

'There's more to life than business,' Ziv says. 'Surely we can have one day off. Let's stay here tomorrow, sleep late, go for a swim.'

Elya is outraged. 'Stay here?'

'One day.'

'What about Lublin?'

'If there is a Lublin.' Ziv contorts his handsome face. 'You go. I'm not.' He's decided to strike. '*Shvita!*' he cries, downing his knapsack.

Elya wishes him dead, then fears his wish might come true.

'This is like a prison march,' Ziv complains. 'It's worse than being locked in a synagogue.'

Kiva scowls at him.

'What's worse than being locked in a synagogue?' Ziv asks. 'I know,' he says. 'Being locked in a synagogue with Elya.'

Elya feels a stinging in his eyes. What about all the times he and Ziv sat together in shul, nudging each other and giggling?

The main synagogue in Mezritsh is a big impressive place with its Holy Ark, its women's gallery, its rows and rows of wooden seats, its double wooden doors, its plaques bearing the names of its benefactors, its squirming boys, and its famous pillars, one in particular carved in the image of a leviathan biting its own tail. If it were ever to let go, a flood would drown the town and all its inhabitants.

Imagine that!

'Let's just get to Lublin already,' Kiva grumbles. 'I thought we were almost there. I thought you said . . . '

'That's right, we should be there already. We're walking too slowly. Obviously.'

'Don't blame me. It's my shoes. I'd like to see you walk in these shoes.' Ziv lifts one up. It's falling to bits. 'Perhaps you can repair it,' he smirks.

'Me?' Elya's offended.

'Didn't your father the *shuster* teach you anything?'

'I told you, I'm a trainee merchant; a scurrier, not a shoemaker.'

There are countless things Elya doesn't know. But this he knows. He will never, ever, be a shoemaker. The *shusters* and *shukhuvargs* of Mezritsh are all poor. Not the poorest, but close to.

The poorest are the *luftmenschen*, urchins and beggars; above them, the rag traders and mattress stuffers; above them, but only slightly, are the scourers and other casual workers; above them, the tannery workers; above them, the haulers, water carriers and shoe-makers; above them, the ordinary tailors, bristleworkers and box-makers; above them, the bakers, millers, hatters and peltmongers; above them, the specialist tailors, butchers, merchants and middle-men; above them, the doctors, lawyers and rabbis, naturally.

Factory owners sit on the very top of the heap. So who cares? Elya cares. He created this list. At ten, he wants to be a joke-maker. Perhaps he could set up a stall and sell jokes. Or curses. For jokes he's thinking, dry. For curses, unusual. Not the familiar *shtetl* curses he hears every day, wishing fire, cholera, worms. His would have to be special. Or maps. He could sell maps. He loves maps and can draw the outlines of Bessarabia, Bucovina, and the Kingdom of Galicia without even looking at his atlas. But where's the money in that?

Whatever job Elya chooses, he'll toil energetically, never give credit, keep tidy accounts and work his way to the top.

What about the deathbed promise you made to your father, Elya?

Well, what about it?

You swore an oath.

XV

'Once upon a time,' Elya tells his friends as they sit around their campfire on the road to Lublin, 'I was kidnapped.'

'Kidnapped?' Ziv sits up.

'By the evil *shuster* of Biale.'

'No!'

'My father was sick, probably delirious when he signed the papers apprenticing me there.'

Ziv can't believe it. 'Biale Shoes? That's a *shtupping* big factory.'

'My mother wanted to keep me home but I was grabbed off the street, carried to Biale in a sack, threatened with a cudgel and set to work toiling long hours in a half-flooded cellar with other *nebekeh kinder*.'

Elya has often imagined how it would have been.

'One boot passed through nine children. Toe cappers, throat liners, eyeleteers, welters, vampers, heelers, quarterers, insolers and outsolers. I was an outsoler. Using an iron plate operated by a hand crank I pressed rivets into outsoles all day. The light was poor. The room was cold. And a *gantseh* steam-powered cutting machine made a terrible noise. In the end, my mother and the Mezritsher rabbi rescued me.'

But is it true?

From his sickbed, his father has indeed organised a shoemaking apprenticeship for young Elya in Biale. Soon the papers, called indentures, arrive to be signed, then notarised in the marketplace.

Once this has occurred, Elya's life will be well and truly over. He's only ten years old at the time. What can he do but run away? He knows where Klara hides the housekeeping and helps himself.

The night wagon to Warsaw leaves from a nearby inn. Heading into the wind, young Elya walks up Brisker Street past the workshops (once a Russian military barracks), the horse stables, a soap factory, a slaughterhouse, a dairy, a lumber mill (sawdust flying), and a blacksmith's. To reach the inn, young Elya must pass both the Old Cemetery on one side of the road, where the old gravestones hide under a tangle of leaves, and the New Cemetery on the other, where the newly dead are buried. The dead, old and new, are said to rise up after dark to pray in the shuls of Mezritsh.

Young Elya looks around. It isn't dark enough for the dead yet. Is it?

It is!

He begins to walk faster, labouring through frozen mud because it's winter, stumbling in his haste. All at once, he feels a hand on his shoulder, a jostle at his elbow. He turns, but there's no one there. Darkness envelops him and he starts to run, not towards the inn but the other way. At his back, pouring through the gates of the New Cemetery and the Old Cemetery, and billowing onto the roadway, the dead chase after.

Panting, chest heaving, arms pumping, feet pounding, young Elya runs back, past the blacksmith's, the lumber mill (sawdust flying), the dairy, the slaughterhouse, the soap factory, the horse stables, the workshops (once a Russian military barracks), and rounds the bend onto his own street at last.

The headstones in the Old Cemetery, the *alter besoylem*, which are crumbling, and those in the New Cemetery, the *nay besoylem*, which are new, will be cut down in the not-too-distant future and used as paving stones beneath the feet, or grindstones to sharpen muddy tools, to humiliate both the living and the dead. This is something Elya would find hard to believe. But it will happen one day when he's middle-aged. If he lives that long. He should live that long! Or maybe not.

Young Elya slinks home and replaces the money before Klara notices it's gone. Due to his father's worsening condition, the apprenticeship is forgotten. Elya goes to school. Comes home. Waits for something else to happen.

Meanwhile on the vanishing road to Lublin, Ziv starts to tell a joke and Elya stares at him with wounded eyes. Jokes are Elya's job.

'A man and a woman are out walking. The woman says she needs a pee. She goes behind a bush and drops her untervesh. The man, feeling desire, puts his hand through the bush and touches something dangling between her legs. "Have you changed into a man?" he cries. "No," she says, "I've changed my mind and decided to hobn a drek."'

Kiva and Elya are silent. Maybe shocked. The idea of girls doing their business behind a bush is disgusting.

Then Kiva laughs.

Elya looks at him in astonishment. Ziv waits for Elya to laugh too. Well, he won't. Why should he?

'You're a prude,' Ziv tells him.

'Prudent,' Elya gets up and walks away.

'Not even a prude,' Ziv calls after him, 'a prune.'

'What's the connection between a friend and a tree?' Elya calls back.

'I don't know. And I don't care,' Ziv replies.

'They both fall over when you strike them with an axe.'

'That's not funny.'

'It's not meant to be.'

Ziv – may he piss bird cherry cordial, in other words, blood – beckons Kiva and draws him close. They sit together whispering. Later, when Ziv goes off to hobn a drek himself, Kiva follows. Making violent efforts to evacuate, he'll do himself an injury. Then, prompted by Ziv, Kiva agrees to continue the story of King Solomon and the rock-cutting worm, one of the so-called ten Jewish wonders of the world. According to Kiva, to capture the worm, King Solomon's men must first find the woodcock's nest which is filled with the woodcock's young, and cover it with a *shtikeleh* glass.

'A *shtik fun glaz*? What for?' asks Elya.

'So that when the woodcock returns, she can see her young, but cannot reach them.'

'Woodcock,' says Ziv with wonder, imagining a bird with a beak like the sharp toe of a Polish boot.

'Hitting her head again and again and scraping her feet on the glass, the mother woodcock panics and calls for the worm to come and break the glass.'

'I thought the worm was already hidden in the nest,' says Elya.

'Well this day he wasn't,' says Kiva.

'Woodcocks eat worms,' says Elya.

They also eat spiders, caterpillars, fly larvae and small snails. But Kiva knows nothing about actual woodcocks, bulky birds with short pink legs. Nor does Elya. Nor Ziv.

'When the worm appears, Solomon's men grab him, put him in a box lined with cotton wool and take him away.'

'Where to?'

'To live on a pillow in King Solomon's bedchamber.'

'Is that it? What about his teeth?'

'It is said by some that the worm has no teeth. That it cuts through stone with its eyes.'

'Eyes?' Ziv is disappointed.

Then Kiva, having told the story without sneezing once, sneezes. On Ziv. And Ziv, without stopping to think, punches him, a long, looping punch, right on the nose, followed by rapid jabs to the side of his head.

Ziv's unable to explain the rage he feels, which has been building. A Jew with a Cossack inside him, poor Ziv is living on *drek*, stuck with *mieskiet* Shayna, *shmucky* Elya, *shlubby* Kiva, *shlocky* brushes, *farkakta* shoes and no beard.

Kiva's chin hits the ground and he lies there as if dead until Ziv hauls him up again. He gives Kiva a twisting pinch on the arm and a few more for good measure, then tells him to get lost. And Kiva meekly slinks away, blood trickling from his nose.

Thinking he might die from Ziv's beatings, Kiva remembers Mindel; the bed they slept in; the *shtul* they sat on; the *tepekh* made of china where they did their business.

'Hands up!' Ziv cries. And Kiva screams, but his gaze is blank and dull.

When Kiva unpacks his feather pillow and arranges it at the head of his bedroll, Ziv watches closely. He's been eyeing it since day one. 'I have a bad neck,' he now says. 'Can I borrow your pillow?'

'This pillow?'

'Just for tonight.'

'It's not an ordinary pillow. The feathers inside have been steam-cured.'

'So? I'm not going to open it.'

'Plucked from live geese. It's only for people with allergies. It's not for sitting on.'

'And why would I do that?'

'You know why. Haemorrhoids,' he whispers.

'I'm just going to lay my head on it. That's all. And I have allergies.'

'You do?' A prickle of suspicion. 'OK. But you must promise me something in return.'

'I won't sit.'

'Something else.'

'What else?'

'You won't hit me again. Not so hard.'

'I thought you liked it.'

'I don't like it so hard.'

'I promise.'

'And promise you won't talk loosely any more.'

'I don't know what you mean. Loosely? Like what? Freely? Openly? Truthfully? Can you give me an example?'

'You know like what.'

Ziv winks at Elya. 'Not until you tell me.'

'No more profanity!'

'Or what? Will a demon take me?' Ziv scoffs, upsetting Kiva, who drops his prayer book and immediately retrieves it with various benedictions.

'I'll die without swearing,' Ziv pretends to die, staggering around, grabbing his neck as if choking and rolling his eyes. Falling to the ground, he shudders once and lies still. 'OK I promise,' he says jumping up again. 'No more loose talk.'

'Or *zetz*?'

'No more jabs, punches or slaps,' he vows.

Then Kiva sneezes again, lightly spattering the pages of his prayer book, and loses his place. Finds his place. Starts to pray. Stops. He has forgotten to wash his hands. Blames Elya for hoarding water. Takes up his prayer book again, kisses it, but that's as far as he gets. What's wrong with him? He recites the morning prayer in the afternoon, the afternoon prayer in the evening, the evening prayer not at all. He'll surely be punished, rolling in thorns for eternity.

In the night, when no one is looking, Ziv caresses Kiva's pillow, moving it from under his head to under his lower parts, rocking back and forth on it. 'Libka,' he moans. Soon after, he's asleep, snoring loudly. Elya watches him bitterly. Without his pillow, Kiva also lies awake.

Midnight by Kiva's gold watch. Ziv's snoring grows louder. Elya and Kiva turn him over, pinch his nose, stuff a shoe rag in his mouth. 'Prop him up,' Kiva says. Nothing helps. If only Elya could snore, he'd snore louder than Ziv. Ziv's snoring begins as a faint, husky sound progressing to a stuttering, heavy gasp. A sound that stops and starts without warning, a rough vibration, a buzzing that dies and swells.

In the distance, fireflies and other luminous insects flicker between the trees. Or is it Cossacks lighting their Russian cigarettes? Fireflies, Elya decides. He's not Kiva. Before lying down again, he places his axe beside his bedroll, just in case; their water flask, his purse, walking stick and map under his bedroll. He lies uncomfortably on top of all these things. No wonder he can't sleep. Can you die from not sleeping? Tossing in his bedroll, he remembers the story of Abimelech and the trees. First the people love Abimelech, then they hate him. Perhaps the people misunderstood his intentions. They thought he was a bad leader, doing bad things. But perhaps he had a plan in mind that would benefit everyone, if only they could see it. Maybe Abimelech was just a man with vision surrounded by the blind? Getting up, Elya finds and buffs his lucky coin. Everything will come right, he tells himself. Lublin cannot be far away. He takes out his notebook, smooths down a page.

He wants to write the date but he's lost track.

'*Burnt kasha for dinner,*' he writes. '*Too hot and too tired to eat much. Except Ziv.*'

'What are you doing?' asks Kiva, still awake, nose swelling.

'Mercantile notes for the Uncle.'

'His clerks do that.'

'Well I'm doing it. Anyway, I can't sleep.'

'Ask Adoshem to help,' suggests Kiva. Then he sneezes. Every sneeze an agony with his injured nose. 'You can speak to him like a friend. Say, "Adoshem, I'm tired. Can you help me?" He's like a father. You can put your head on his shoulder. Ask him to send you sweet dreams.'

'OK,' Elya says warily.

'Adoshem will make everything all right,' says Kiva.

Moments later, Kiva's asleep.

Elya?

Still tossing.

Ziv?

Still snoring.

Elya could easily kill Ziv now. His axe, hardened in brine, then tempered over an open fire, lies at his side. He feels for the handle. Ziv is not a friend. He's a traitor and a saboteur. Elya lifts his axe experimentally, then puts it down. Maybe he falls asleep after that because a moment later, sitting beside him on the ground, Elya sees the Uncle. The Uncle, whose face is a mother's face; whose hair is the finest bristles which come up from the washing; whose temples are whitefish dipped in schnapps; whose skin is as soft as goat-kid trousers; whose teeth resemble real teeth; whose nose is a large Jewish nose; whose legs are as white as stubble-fed geese; whose hips are children reciting blessings; whose brush case is small but tightly packed. How beautiful are his feet in shoes!

'Kill them both,' says Uncle Velvel. 'Those shovel thieves!'

'Both of them?' protests Elya. 'I thought just Ziv.'

'That's what a real businessman would do.'

'But Kiva's your nephew.'

'Business is not a brotherhood,' says the Uncle, before disappearing in a puff of smoke. Then Elya's father Usher of blessed memory appears at his workbench hammering. He complains about ready-made shoes and a machine that can peg the soles of two shoes to two uppers in less than two minutes. It's a dream Elya has had before. *Zeyn tata* wants him to take hold of the hammer, but Elya resists. 'One hammer blow,' his father pleads, putting the tool in Elya's hand. 'You promised.'

*

On the day he dies, 14 November 1903, Elya's father is in a state of excessive excitement, which is the false energy that seems to mask, but actually precedes, a consumptive's passing. In his last frantic hours, hands beating the air, then scraping, digging and thrashing, as if swimming against a current in the Krzna River, Usher tries again and again to climb out of bed without waiting to be helped.

The sky that November day is bright and light with fast-moving clouds. Usher cries for the window to be opened. But there is no window in the small dark sickroom he occupies. Klara feeds him a spoonful of sugar to ease his pain, fear and sadness, but Elya's father has difficulty swallowing. She licks a fingertip, puts it into the sugar bag, then lets her husband suck.

Rifka and Elya are sent for. Fishel can't be found.

Both children hang back. Klara, who is holding baby Zusa, nudges them from behind. With the toe of her shoe, she pushes a little glazed bedpan under the bed and out of sight. Usher, however, has ceased producing urine and the bedpan is dry.

'My son the shoemaker,' Usher looks at Elya with loving eyes. And Elya, barely ten years old, finds himself agreeing to spend his life, his one precious life, making and repairing shoes like his father. He actually says the promise word. He even kisses the tips of his fingers as his father requires and lays them on his heart. Seeing this, Usher smiles and reaches out for his glass of tea which he can no longer lift on his own. Holding the drink to Usher's lips, Elya cannot help but remember the great expanse of his father's back, his arms like iron bars, or so it seemed once upon a time. Or sitting on his father's knee, head against his big chest listening to his heart beat like a drum. If only he would ask for a joke.

'A man is hit by a carriage on Lubliner Street and the doctor is sent for. When he arrives, Herr Doktor, *kneeling beside the dying man, sees there is nothing he can do. "Are you comfortable?" asks the doctor sympathetically.*

"Eh," replies the injured man, "I make a living."'

On the endless road to Lublin, Elya should be dreaming of getting ahead, of buying and selling, of paintbrushes in bales of one thousand, of brush wagons, purchase orders, *monopolkas*. Instead he's dreaming of his father and shoes. Dreams are not important, Elya decides. Real life is. He will tell no one of his nightmare. He's not Kiva.

Meanwhile Kiva's pestering Adoshem. 'Talk to me, my dove,' he begs. 'Tell me why you've sent me on this terrible journey.'

But Adoshem no longer speaks to men. The age of prophets is over; everyone knows that.

It's very late. Trees stir in the darkness. And there's another sound, a soft rustling.

Ziv is also awake. Sitting up and thinking himself unobserved, he is stuffing leftover kasha into his mouth.

XVI

The following day they walk without stopping. But no Village of Fools is found. No Lublin Uplands. No Lublin.

'*Baroch ata Adonai . . .*' Elya actually prays for Lublin, the suburbs of Lublin at least. But his prayers are not answered. They encounter nothing and no one. Then suddenly the outlines of buildings appear in the distance. Is it Lublin at last?

No, it's some sleepy, nearly deserted village not indicated on Elya's map. No marketplace, not many houses, few people. Nothing but the smell of burning feathers.

That night they choose another campsite and Elya spends another sleepless night. Then they're on the road again. How can this be? They've been walking for days. Only 102 kilometres from Mezritsh, Lublin has been harder to find than King Solomon's worm. Ignoring the flattened worms he sees, or those shrivelling in the heat, Ziv is still searching for this stone-ingesting marvel. Perhaps it's all that's keeping him going.

It's still early. Back home in Mezritsh, morning fires are just being kindled. On Szmulowizna Street, Libka's father is lighting his first cigarette of the day. Occasionally, Libka appears to Elya as if in a dream and he remembers the last time they were together before he set off to seek his fortune on the road to Lublin. Elya, in a clean shirt, hair carefully combed and dressed with oil, sits beside Libka on the banks of the Krzna River in Mezritsh, eating prunes. The shore is lined with birch trees, evergreens beyond. Big frogs croak in the sandy shallows, finger frogs beneath the bushes. In the thickets, birds whistle. This could be a fairy tale except for the mud, dried hard this time of year and turned to dust.

Elya brags about his heavy backpack. Not a girl's pack. A proper pack. He shows Libka his precious map and points out the route.

'So far,' she marvels, but with a hint of reproach.

'It's difficult to get ahead unless you go on the road,' he explains cautiously.

Then he shows her his account book and tells her about the paintbrushes he will sell, how they are constructed and so forth.

She sinks into his words, a sweet, eager expression on her face.

'Under the ferrule, a little pocket holds the paint.'

'Ferrule,' she silently mouths.

They've never been alone together. They ought not to be alone tonight. But since Elya is leaving, they've been allowed. A long silence grows longer. He has to say something. A joke? No, not a joke. His shoulder bumps her shoulder. 'Sorry,' he says. Then she asks for another prune.

'*Zay azoy gut*,' she says, holding out her small hand.

He wonders if she will come with him to America one day or if he should send for her once he's established like many men do. Should he even mention it now? It's on the tip of his tongue to say something. But he stops himself. What if she doesn't want to leave Mezritsh? He tries anyway. 'Sometimes,' he begins, 'I have a longing . . .'

She looks at him intensely.

'A longing,' he starts again, ' . . . for elsewhere.'

'Elsewhere?' This is not what she expects to hear.

He decides not to press the point but to wait and see.

They laugh about her friend Shayna.

'Shayna wants to marry you.'

'Really?'

'She hates me.'

'Don't say that.'

As they sit staring out across the river, the sky slowly darkens above the treetops on the opposite shore. Libka will remember this evening for the rest of her short life. 'It's uncomfortable at home,' she stammers. 'Too many sisters. Not enough beds. My uncle . . .' she laughs. Elya laughs too. But what she's attempting to tell him isn't a laughing matter. She eats her prune, delicately sucking the pit, then carefully spitting it into her hand and dropping it on the ground.

With the toe of his shoe, Elya guides it closer and closer, and when he thinks she isn't looking, bends down, picks it up and puts it in his pocket. Something that has been in her mouth, he feels almost faint. There isn't much more time. Soon Libka will set off for home. Her father, smoking one cigarette after another, is already waiting for her in front of their house that no longer stands on swampy Szmulowizna Street, the poorest street in Mezritsh.

Solemnly, Elya walks Libka home, without drawing her close or even putting an arm lightly around her shoulders. What's wrong with him? She's beautiful and willing. A cattle car is just pulling out of Mezritsh Station. They both hold their noses laughing. Elya is vaguely embarrassed by the smell. He stops walking. She stops walking. He turns towards her, pecks her on the cheek.

'I won't tell,' she whispers.

But he's already moving away. Then he turns back. 'Libka,' he murmurs, holding out his hand. When she takes it, instead of caressing her, he practises his new handshake, a money handshake such as businessmen and merchants employ.

Shortly after Elya goes on the road, Libka's house will catch fire. While her mother's back is turned, a spark will jump from the brazier on which she cooks and into a barrel filled with ropes; or maybe her father, smoking one cigarette after another, will throw a butt aside before properly extinguishing it; or her bachelor uncle will be carelessly burning grain to ferment his own alcohol; or a candle will be knocked over by her lively sisters, and all Elya's dreams of Libka will be reduced to flying cinders.

It is said that a huge cloud of ash covered the whole of Szmulowizna Street after the fire, like a coat of grey fur. But of course, on this night, when Elya and Libka part so chastely, nothing's happened yet and the Mezritsher Fire Brigade have got their feet up, eating kreplach, which are dumplings.

Only Libka's uncle survives.

In Mezritsh, the gossips will say that Elya's abandoned fiancée, dosed with St John's wort for sadness, set fire to the house herself.

A tisheleh, a benkele, a baleboosteh bet sich zu zein.

This is all Libka ever wanted.

Perhaps it was jealous Shayna who set the fire.

Meanwhile, Elya, with no Lublin, hates his friends. He has no friends. Certainly not Ziv, or Kiva. He doesn't need friends. The Uncle has no friends. Only creditors.

Kiva, with no pillow (Ziv hasn't returned it), hates the road; the side of the road; the fields beyond the road; his big *pupik*; the shameful things he has done (she's his sister, his sister!) and whatever punishment Ziv dishes out, he deserves. But not so hard!

Ziv, with no beard, a maggoty knapsack and disintegrating shoes, hates pale-faced, weaker boys; the Tsar who dissolved the second Duma; and *farkakta* rich men with their camels. He fantasises about the emptying of Lubliner Street and the handing over of fur coats, gold watches, fine furniture. A great storm is coming that will sweep through rich men's houses and carry everything away. He also hates his cousin Kiva who is nearly rich, and Elya, who is not rich but wants to be.

One day he will set their beards on fire.

There are vapours through the night and heat lightning. How many days have they been on the road? They've lost count. It's overcast. Still very hot. Soon the weather must break. The empty sky takes on a white appearance and leaves hang motionless on the trees.

Waiting for Kiva and Ziv to rouse themselves in the morning, Elya packs and repacks his knapsack. Crapsack, Ziv calls it. Then Elya takes out his notebook again. *'Slept ill,'* he writes. Perhaps he will not sleep until they reach Lublin. But then, Lublin sleep! He gets up, lifts his tarp and squashes it into his crapsack without folding.

'I like the way you folded that.' The Uncle comes up behind him. Then Elya must do it again. Elya does not need to check their provisions because there are no provisions. Everything squandered. Nothing left. They will have to find food somewhere.

After Kiva rises, they sit in silence, watching Ziv sleep. How could a person sleep so much?

'Ziv!' Elya hollers. 'Get the fuck up.'

Kiva stares at Elya in dismay.

Ziv opens one eye.

'Get up.' Elya prods him with his foot, not gently.

'You mean now?'

'I'm leaving,' says Elya, 'with or without you.'

All he needs to do is put on his shoes.

Then Ziv's dressed and ready in no time.

Ziv dressed and ready? What gives?

'Now we're waiting for you,' Ziv complains, while Elya unpacks his backpack and unrolls his bedroll looking for his shoes.

'I haven't seen them,' Ziv turns to Kiva. 'Have you?'

'My father made those shoes,' Elya stirs the campfire ashes with the fallen branch of a tree. Nothing there. Heads off to search the lake. Comes back empty-handed.

'You'll have to wrap your feet in rags,' Ziv calls out to him. 'Wait a minute. Are these yours?' He lifts Elya's shoes from the long grass. 'Right here all along.'

Elya glares at him. 'If you've damaged them . . . '

'Me? I'm admiring them.' Ziv squeezes the toes as if to assess the quality of the leather. Ziv's own shoes are in tatters, but Kiva has a spare pair.

'You brought two pairs of shoes?'

'Three. Four, if you count my slippers.'

Bursting with indignation, Ziv tries on Kiva's spare shoes. 'They pinch,' he complains. 'Thanks, but no thanks.'

Meanwhile, repacking his bedroll, Elya finds his lost shovel. 'A miracle,' he cries out. Is it really his shovel?

It is!

'Who put it there?' Ziv asks with a bewildered smile.

'Adoshem?' suggests Kiva.

'Demons,' Ziv opines.

Ziv, thinks Elya.

It's another day. A new beginning. Thinking their journey almost over, Elya is actually hopeful, hopeful and nostalgic. 'These are the best of times. Days we will never forget,' he says.

'Although we might try,' says Ziv.

'Try and try,' says Kiva. There's dried blood around his swollen nose and black and blue marks on his arms. He looks down the road and grimaces.

'Don't worry,' Elya reassures him. 'There are doctors in Lublin who specialise in noses, broken, ill-shaped, or Jewish.'

On the road, it is hotter, closer. Beneath a sultry sky, the landscape, a flat monotonous plain covered with rough dry grass, interests no one. Ziv and Elya strip to the waist. Even Kiva takes off his overshirt. He drops it. Then picks it up. Dropping things is a sure sign that a fit is coming. Soon he'll be falling to the ground right in front of his friends, his arms and legs going in all directions.

A newly mowed field is hazy in the overcast sunlight, buzzing with insects and the birds that feed on them. They pass a church, its doors open wide. 'Don't look,' Kiva calls out. 'You'll go blind.'

Too late. They've looked. Elya cannot identify anything he sees inside. 'Now we're in for it,' Kiva predicts. 'I saw a lamb,' he cries in dismay, 'with a crook between its legs.'

Up ahead, the road forks. Elya wants to go right. But a large red-eyed dog is barring their way. When it sees them, the dog begins to growl low down in its throat, then snaps and snarls aggressively. When Ziv approaches the animal, Kiva opens his mouth, screams, then starts to cough.

'It's just a dog.'

Der hundt barks wildly at Ziv, foaming at the mouth.

Ziv backs away.

Suddenly there's a long, sharp whistle from a nearby field and the big farm dog turns and runs off towards the sound.

A large, sandy marketplace, in a small Polish village not on Elya's map, looks promising. They decide to stop and set up their wares. They open their suitcase and display their paintbrushes, which come in many shapes and sizes. A small brush for window frames, sashes and sills; a medium-sized brush for doors and cabinets; a large brush for walls. '*Dzien dobry*,' Elya greets every potential customer. 'A new brush will make painting easier. Even a child could do it,' he cries in a mixture of Yiddish and bad Polish, attracting a crowd. 'I use these brushes myself. Good clean brushes. No broken bristles. Ideal for the house painter. Long-lasting in both square and tapered versions. Well-balanced. Well-priced. Quality-controlled with a special seal of approval from a licensed brush inspector.' (This is untrue but sounds good.) 'Durable, all-purpose brushes. Made in Mezritsh. Home of the bristle.'

'The brush for Everyman,' Ziv puts in.

'A newly painted wall for the Jewish holidays,' Kiva suggests. But those who listen are not Jews. 'Buy one, get one half price,' Elya adds. 'OK. Buy two, get one free. Not many left. Everything must go. I can't *shlep* brushes back to Mezritsh,' he exclaims.

They sell not one paintbrush. So, not the Village of Fools after all, where *nebachs* will buy anything. Maybe the Village of the Dead, where no Mezritsher merchant has ever made a sale. The trestle they have rented, in the only space available, stands under a sign reading 'SWÓJ DLA SWEGO'.

What could that mean? Only Ziv knows and he's not telling.

Soon they're on the parched road to Lublin again. They have not walked very far when they encounter a distinctive smell. Stewed prunes and pastry. Elya looks around in dismay. Could there be two Prune Towns? This time Kiva takes no notice. He's lost his appetite. But Elya's worried. Are they walking in circles? He struggles to stay calm. But fear enters his heart. Where's the Village of Fools and why's it taking so long to reach Lublin?

'Are we almost there?' Kiva asks.

Dogs flicker between the trees.

Ziv shakes a stick at a red-eyed mongrel similar to one they've seen before. Every direction, and every dog, looks the same. 'Where are we?' Elya wants to ask, but his stupid pride won't let him. More dogs. More trees. Then no trees. Or dogs. Only horse fields and cow fields as far as the eye can see.

'Are we there yet?' asks Kiva.

Ziv hails an old-fashioned pedlar, his wares strapped to his back, his feet wrapped in rags. '*Vas mahkhsta?*' Ziv enquires. 'Is this the road to Lublin?'

'Lublin?' The man looks confused. 'Never heard of it.'

Could this be Ziv's father?

Elya hurries Ziv on. That type, Elya's thinking, gives our esteemed profession a bad name.

'I just wanted to say hello,' Ziv protests.

'We're already late.'

'How much longer?' asks Kiva.

A line of blind *schnorrers* with upturned eyelids is chanced upon next, shuffling along. The foremost blind beggar, led by a child reciting blessings, is tall and thin with pointy ears like Ziv's, sharp teeth like Ziv's, Ziv's clever vulpine expression, and a wispy beard, if you could call it a beard. Perhaps this is Ziv's father.

'*Tata?*'

When Elya pulls him away, Ziv bristles. 'What's happened to you Elya? He looked a good fellow.' And before he can stop him, Ziv thrusts his hand inside the purse Elya carries around his waist, extracts a coin, runs after the beggar and gives it to him.

Later, Elya will find that the coin Ziv has given the beggar is his lucky pfennig.

Does he want Ziv dead? Not really dead, he decides, just disappeared, rounded up, taken away.

Kiva watches miserably as his friends argue. 'Let's have a song,' he proposes, and bursts into *Ein Keloheinu*, a rousing Jewish hymn. Soon they are all singing lustily as they march down the road.

'*Ein Keloheinu, Ein Kadoneinu,*
Ein k'malkeinu, Ein K'moshieinu.'

They're just boys after all.

XVII

They arrive the following day, or is it the day after that, at a good-sized village. Shall they try to sell their brushes in the village marketplace? It's late in the day and the road into the village, rutted from the weight of many carts, is empty. They cross a large unoccupied square littered with marketplace rubbish and spilled grain. Even the hawkers with their trays of boiled eggs and smoked nuts are gone.

'We're too late,' Ziv laughs.

Elya looks at him with loathing. He should have listened to the Uncle and used the axe.

Returning to the never-ending road, they pass trees consumed by blight; animal *drek*; dead animals; thorn bushes; thornier bushes; villages not on Elya's map; and peasants harvesting in sun-baked fields who ignore them, or gaze at them aggressively. Where are the valleys, the groves, the streams gently flowing, that they encountered only days ago? Or was it weeks? Surely not weeks?

A breath of wind dies before reaching them. Even the dust is scorched, bringing to mind the famous famine of 1891, when seeds would not germinate and a gritty wind blew the topsoil away. A dog lying across the road doesn't even look up when they pass. There's no shade. The sun hammers on their backs, on the tops of their heads, and in their eyes. Blinded, they stumble along, *plotzing* and *shvitzing*; *shvitzing* and *plotzing*. The hum of insects is driving them mad.

'Pray for rain,' Kiva is told.

'May it rain like a mother's tears,' Kiva prays.

'This is your uncle's fault, sending us out without a wagon,' Ziv complains. 'We could be snoring in a wagon right now.'

And Kiva agrees.

'A wagon?' Elya is scandalised. Only senior merchants have wagons.

Kiva falls behind again, babbling about Adoshem's white fire.

'Which is what?'

Elya doesn't even wait for an answer. He's tired of waiting. He tries and fails to ignore a pain at his temples and between his eyes. His pack seems heavier. Has someone been filling it with stones? Naturally, he suspects Ziv. The brush case, once such a privilege to carry, is now awkward and burdensome. Demoralised, he cannot for a moment remember why he's here.

'How much longer?' Kiva whines. He lags behind Ziv, who lags behind Elya.

'Let's stop for a minute,' Ziv cries. 'Why hurry?'

Elya stops for a minute and seethes. He remembers walking home from the marketplace in Mezritsh one evening with Mordy. There was a real friend, despite his complaining. All the way from Synagogue Street to the New Path, from Railway Street to Swiniaczer Lane, Mordy complains. A wedding has been hastily arranged for him to avoid conscription, but Mordy would rather lose a finger than marry. He'll have to get a job to support a wife. How will he ever become a mathematician then?

'What did the constipated mathematician do?' Elya asks him.

'I don't know,' says Mordy. 'What?'

'He worked it out with a pencil!'

Skinny Mordy laughs so hard his trousers fall down.

'Question,' Elya jokes. *'What does the zero say to the eight?'*

'I don't know,' says Mordy.

'Nice belt!'

More laughter.

In the distance, a train pulling a long row of closed boxcars leaves Mezritsh Station, the engine venting plumes of smoke that rise over the embankment and feather the air. They pause to watch as the hills leading into the Zahajk Forest turn blue. Then walk on. *'Have you heard about the mathematician who was afraid of negative numbers? He'd stop at nothing to avoid them.'*

Mordy laughs so much he forgets his *tsores*. Then they hear music coming from afar. Elya turns to Mordy. Should they be wary? Perhaps it's the *Khappers* luring boys into their grasp with the help of unscrupulous musicians. A boy's fate, once captured, is so terrible and mysterious, no one wants to discuss it, and both Elya and Mordy have only the vaguest notions steeped in dread. In the autumn, boys with good feet, normal heartbeats and sane minds must stay indoors, get married, lose a finger, or else. But it's not autumn, so they decide to follow the sound. Soon they find themselves on an unfamiliar street where a crowd has gathered around an opened window. From within a plain front room, no bigger than most, comes the music of an orchestra. How is this possible? They press closer and see a marvel – a turntable cranked by hand, causing beautiful music to come from a large tin horn. Before long, people are dancing on the pavement, praising with delight the gramophone. Mezritshers can hardly wait for the future which is bound to be full of such wonders.

Elya and Mordy begin to dance together too. And why not? Everyone else is.

It's the last time Elya will see Mordy in this life.

Then Elya is back on the road with Kiva and Ziv. Ziv draws Kiva aside and they whisper together, while Elya walks on, turning sharply from time to time to watch them, alert to their plans to obstruct him. Imagine his surprise, expecting comradery, beholding wretched betrayal instead. Or is he mistaken? Susceptible to irrational suspicions? According to the alienist, *Herr Doktor* Sigmund Freud, repressed infantile wishes and sexual disturbances in childhood are important factors in the development of paranoia. Another practitioner, *Herr Doktor* Carl Jung, takes a different view. What does a patient want to achieve, he asks, by the creation of a paranoid delusion? One doctor looks to the past for clues; the other to the future. They'll both meet soon for the first time in Vienna, and argue.

'Are we there yet?' asks Kiva.

An old, sick dog wandering down the road overtakes them. 'We'll never get to Lublin at this rate,' cries Elya desperately. 'Can't you walk any faster? Race you?' But Kiva can't run. And Ziv? Similarly disinclined.

'Don't mind Elya,' Ziv says to Kiva. 'He's got *shpilkes.*' And they all laugh. Even Elya who's got ants in his pants; even Ziv whose anger is raging out of control; even Kiva who seems to be shivering despite the heat, who's coughing and sneezing and dropping whatever he picks up.

Now Ziv has a pebble in his shoe and they must stop while he sits and unfastens the showy buckle, takes off the shoe, rattles it, and peers inside. 'I can't walk with a pebble in my shoe, can I?'

Eventually, they regain the road. While light-stepping Elya lopes ahead, his feet barely touching the ground, Kiva hobbles, shambles, shuffles, and stumbles, and Ziv in his indecent *shikhlek* with their buckles and bits, lolls, lounges and sprawls as he walks, if you could call it walking, alongside him.

'Isn't there an inn or café along this road where we can stop for refreshment?' Kiva enquires.

'Three friends stop at a roadside café for three glasses of tea,' says Elya.

'Spare us,' begs Kiva.

"'Make sure the glass is clean," one tells the waiter.

"Three teas," the waiter returns with their drinks. "Who asked for the clean glass?"'

The oldest joke in Jewish Poland.

Any laughter? Elya leans forward straining his ears. But hears nothing.

When he can afford it, Elya will purchase an Octophone, which is more effective than earlier attempts at hearing amplification. Although advertised as portable, the Octophone will be heavy to carry around, weighing seven kilos, which means little to Elya who's familiar only with Russian Imperial measurements.

'Are we almost there?' cries Kiva again.

In time, they come to a dry river. Parched cattails, reeds and marsh grass line the shore, beyond which is another peasant village: one street; one whimpering child standing in front of one broken door; one burned-out carriage; one old horse. Where are all the bustling Jewish villages? The people numerous as herrings, laughing, crying, arguing, buying and selling? Where's the smell, in every house, of beetroots boiling at dusk?

There's a dead dog swarming with flies at the side of the road and Kiva must be led past it. Elya has the sinking feeling he's seen it before, but all big farm dogs look alike. Don't they?

Ziv's the only one brave enough to approach it. He bends over the animal which leaps up and snaps at his face, then falls back and expires in earnest.

Dead grass, dead trees, dead dogs. Wherever Elya looks something is dead or dying. The road forks again. A long moment of bewilderment, fear and indecision.

'This looks familiar,' says Ziv. 'Have we been here before? Holy *drek*,' he cries, 'I think we have.'

Overhead, the first small clouds sweep across the sky. More familiar fields, stooks, peasants, trees. Elya blinks to moisten his eyes. He stops, turns, fumbles for his map, then stands frozen to the spot.

Ikh bin farloyrn, he thinks. They're not only lost, but really lost. A map does not lie. But still it's perplexing. There must be something wrong. But what? They're following in the footsteps of other venerable merchants. How can that be wrong?

'Show me where we are on the map,' Ziv insists.

'There.'

'There? Are you sure? Who drew this map?'

Elya gives Ziv a hard look. Steadying himself, he brings the map close to his face and looks at it. Could it be that the merchant who drew the map and sold it to Elya for one kopek was playing a trick? Sending Elya and his friends in the wrong direction to avoid competition?

'That's business, son,' Elya hears the Uncle say. 'Business is not a brotherhood.'

Elya loves business and is disappointed and confused. 'I . . . er . . . think we're on the wrong road,' he stammers, at last, vexed and ashamed. Even Adoshem doesn't know where they are. Elya crumples the map in his fist. A fun map, never meant to be taken seriously. Then he straightens it out again, not quite believing he's been duped.

It's late afternoon. They're tired, footsore, disheartened. The dirt road they've been travelling changes to a badly paved road. Irregular stone paving is hard on the feet. Especially Ziv's feet in shoes with soles thin as herring fillets. Picking their way onward, stumbling over every *shteyn*, they hate their lives. What now? In the distance they hear the creak of carriage wheels slowly turning and the clop of horses. Soon, a canvas-covered wagon hung with banners comes into view. It's a Jewish wedding party, complete with a fiddler and a blind accordion player. What could be more fortuitous than that?

The young bride, tiny head, little pointed chin, is weeping. Behind her comes a line of uncles, dancing.

But where's the young bridegroom?

'Join us,' one of the uncles calls out.

'Please,' begs Kiva.

'I'm stopping,' says Ziv.

And Elya uncharacteristically surrenders. Maybe someone in the wedding party can direct them to Lublin. 'Where are we?' he cries as the uncles dance away. 'Is this not the Lublin road?'

In a field, long tables and benches have been set out for eating. There's a platform for musicians and an area for dancing. There are women carrying trays of food: herring with pickled onions, salad in sour dressing, cabbage leaves stuffed with meat and rice, beef tongue, cows' feet, chicken *pulkes*.

'Please partake,' the uncles invite them.

Are they dreaming?

There are trays of glasses filled with schnapps. Ziv reaches eagerly. Swallows in gulps. Waves his glass for more. Kiva has a sip and coughs it up. Has another. Keeps it down.

Elya's first full glass of schnapps. Pinpricks in his throat, flaring up his nose. A rush of well-being. A lopsided smile. Their glasses are filled again and again. '*L'Chayim*,' they cry.

At the table, Ziv stuffs his mouth and his pockets. Elya takes a coin of chocolate wrapped in gold foil. But Kiva can't decide. Prune *rugelach* or prune strudel? The wedding joker, a jester with bells on the heels of his shoes, recites a bawdy lyric in praise of the newlyweds.

But where's the young bridegroom?

The bride cries harder. The bride's mother is also weeping. Ziv, Elya and Kiva laugh at her tears.

One should never laugh at a mother's tears.

*

It's a lively wedding. The beggars are begging. The jester is jesting. The matchmaker is making new matches. Everything but a basket of doves. But where's the young bridegroom? Has he run off? Is that why the bride is weeping?

The rabbi is carried aloft in an armchair. 'Monsieur Rabbi,' Kiva addresses him, lowering his eyes.

While four couples dance an old-fashioned quadrille, doing all the steps in five parts, the uncles (who will die from tumours, hearts, and fatty livers) throw their heads back, hopping up and down in a circle, dancing faster and faster as if caught in the whirlwind of a fan. The bride (who will perish many years later by gas inhalation), dancing alone like a little moth, wants a partner. So where is he, her new husband?

Ziv grabs Elya and they dance together. 'Loosen up,' Ziv complains, 'It's like dancing with a door.' Then he grabs Kiva and whirls him about. Soon Kiva will be sick.

The wedding children sprouting miniature beards run after Ziv, pulling at his clothes. A little girl (electrocuted one day trying to climb a fence) shrieks with delight. The whole party, observes Ziv, even the rabbi's wife (who expires in a cattle car), even the *kinder* (lined up and shot beside the mouth of a ravine), have beards. Elya observes their home-made shoes. Kiva doesn't observe anything. The schnapps has gone right to his head.

Soon it'll be time for the young bridegroom to deliver his oration. But where is he, the *putz*?

'I'll be the bridegroom,' Ziv says, making the rabbi laugh. He performs his *shtek*-swallowing trick again and the whole party is amused. Then he tries on the bride's veil and simpers around, pretending to fall headlong into the cake. He's funnier than the wedding jester (shot while resisting arrest), who gives him the evil eye.

When one of the nuptial beggars in his nuptial rags asks for alms, Elya says no. They're young scurriers watching every kopek.

He'll give to charity when he makes his fortune. The beggar (locked in a burning synagogue) curses Elya loud enough for all to hear.

Well, what's a wedding without a curse?

Shifting and lengthening in a gentle wind, a bank of clouds drifts overhead. Then the wedding jester tells a joke.

'A man walks into a stonecutter's shop. "I want to order a stone for my dear wife," the man says.

"Your wife," says the stonecutter. "I carved a stone for her last year."

"That was my first wife," the man sighs. "I'm talking now about my second wife."

"Second wife," the stonecutter cries, "I didn't know you remarried. Mazel tov!"'

It's the perfect Jewish joke. The guests are all laughing with tears in their eyes.

Ziv, dancing under the trees with a pretty girl (betrayed for a kilo of salt), has never had more fun.

Kiva's asleep behind a bush.

But where's the *chossin*? He must appear soon.

Then an old man with a muddy complexion and a wrinkled face (who'll soon expire from irregular bowel movements) grabs Elya by the arm. The father of the bride, Elya thinks, *kibbutzing*, not dancing. With his feet? Who can dance? A birdseller by trade, he carries a miniature abacus and complains bitterly about business. 'No one's doing much,' he says with an anguished face, and sighs like a man who's lost two wives.

Birds may be slow, thinks Elya, but paintbrushes are always in demand. 'We're headed for the great bazaars of Lublin,' he says. 'Perhaps you can point out the quickest way?'

'Lublin?' The old man looks at him in alarm.

At that moment, the wind picks up, hats fly, and a cloud, shaped like a small fist, appears in the sky. The trees shiver. The sun darkens and the world seems dim. Never mind, they're having fun.

Then a bolt of lightning flashes and the first drops of rain fall on the back of Elya's neck.

The bride has stopped crying, but neither smiles, nor speaks, nor eats but a morsel. There's a hired carriage to take the happy couple away, pulled by a horse wearing a crown of flowers. A youngster (who drowns trying to reach Palestine) is the driver.

'But where's the bridegroom?' Elya asks the corpse-like old man.

'Here,' he replies. 'I'm the bridegroom. Imagine that!'

XVIII

That night the rain comes down in torrents. They've made a hasty camp but no one has thought to bring an umbrella so they huddle under Elya's tarpaulin, their weary sore heads on their knees, fermentation on their breath.

'*On a stormy night, a dying shoemaker asks his wife to send for the priest.*'

'Shut up Elya.'

"*A priest? Have you lost your mind? You're a Jew,*" *she tells him.*

"*Eh,*" *shrugs the dying man.* "*Why disturb the rabbi on a night like this?*"'

All night it rains. In the morning it rains. Noon? It's still raining.

We can't stay here, Elya thinks. The temperature drops. They shiver and moan.

'Let's just go back,' Kiva wheezes.

'Back where?'

'Back home.'

'To Mezritsh?'

'It's not too late,' say Kiva and Ziv.

Elya pictures them stumbling back into town, *shvantzes* between their legs, failures at even the smallest, most basic commercial venture. Uncle Velvel will never trust Elya again.

Everything's wet. But they're ready to go. In the rain. Just one more push, Elya reckons, when Kiva has to pause and pray. 'This is all your fault,' Ziv tells him. 'You prayed for rain. Now ask Adoshem to make it to stop.'

Kiva will try. But where's his prayer book?

Left in the rain.

The road has turned from dust to mud. Their trousers, mud-splattered. Their shoes, mud shoes. 'What's a bit of rain?' asks Elya. It's so dark they can barely see the way ahead. Kiva wants to find an inn.

'Of course,' agrees Elya, who doesn't agree at all, but feels safe in assenting. All this time, they've passed not a single inn. No fear they'll pass one now.

Wishing his mother would appear tempting him with an egg cookie, Kiva plods slowly on. But his mother is in Mezritsh thinking her son is prospering, congratulating herself for sending him on the road.

Kiva believes he has a fever, but neither Elya nor Ziv will put their lips to his forehead as any mother would have done. Maybe he's caught something off Ziv?

'Who me?'

Or Ziv's mother.

'Who her?'

Something she might have brought home from the Jewish Hospital where she works.

'In the kitchen?'

'So?'

The whole place is known to be poisonous in atmosphere.

Mid-afternoon it's as dark as night. Without warning, a carriage comes speeding towards them and they are lost in a blinding spray of road water. 'It never rains like this in Mezritsh,' Ziv observes. They pass a tree split by lightning, then another. 'We must take shelter,' Elya says. Kiva claps his hands together with joy, picturing an inn with a roaring fire. But Elya leads them off the road towards a rocky outcrop. From under this stony ridge, they watch the rain fall in sheets.

'Isn't this cosy?' asks Elya.

It rains harder.

'A heavy summer rain. Nothing more.'

Things fall off trees.

'Imagine how beautiful everything will look after.'

Mud slithers and slides around them.

'The peasants need rain.'

'Shut the *shtup* up!' cries Ziv.

Ziv could have cried 'Zip it!', but the zipper, invented in 1906, does not make its first domestic appearance in Poland until 1923.

Then the wind rises, nearly blowing them off the narrow ledge on which they sit. 'We'll drown,' Kiva hollers.

In Aquatic Park, America, Harry Houdini escapes from chains underwater in fifty-seven seconds.

Even Harry Houdini is said to be, you should pardon the expression, a Jew.

Houdini?

Yes him.

Ziv knows the word hurricane. But there are no hurricanes in Poland. If only they had a radio. They could send a distress signal like the first such cry for help transmitted in 1904. When the wind changes direction, they're drenched. They huddle together for warmth. 'We're all going to die,' Kiva sobs. Will he never smell pastry baking again, or hear his mother with a mortar and pestle crushing almonds and raisins? 'Mindel,' he calls out.

Ziv's affected too, imagining no more inky pamphlets, workers' songs and slogans, or women tempting him to madness. He even recalls his poor home fondly, the remains of a herring on the table, lamps burning the cheapest kerosene and giving off the blackest smoke, his sisters bickering.

'Kreplach,' cries Ziv, remembering his favourite small dumplings.

'Gudgeon in a blanket,' cries Kiva, recalling the battered fish everyone loves to eat.

'*Kishkas*,' cries Ziv.

'*Gehakter* herring on rye bread.'

'*Gefilte* fish and *chrain*.'

'Latkes.'

'Kugel!'

They both look at Elya.

'Soup,' he says.

He could show more enthusiasm. He tries to conjure up a bowl filled with borscht, the ewe's cheese he likes, his mother's face. It's all rather hazy. He imagines himself back home, inhaling the tarry naphthalene smell of the preparations Klara uses to exterminate moths. She opens the door. Gives a shriek of pleasure and surprise when she sees him. He tries to imagine it. But all he can distinctly picture is the Uncle's steel money box, growing smaller and smaller, so that soon it resembles a toy. He tells himself it'll turn out all right. He just has to hang on, stay committed, resist doubts. But try as he might, he can no longer hear the clink of coins, the sound which has been driving him on. He strains his ears. Nothing.

His mother is home lamenting. She never wanted him to go. In addition to wandering into a pogrom, she fears her son might be converted by roaming priests or conscripted into the Tsar's army and converted by force. Klara has a terror of conversion and spends the little free time she has reading books about apostates. She owns a whole series of Yiddish romances concerning foolish Jewish youngsters seduced by Russians. And where does one meet Russians? On the road. And not only that, there's noxious air, poisoned wells, bad coins, loose women, libertines, gentiles who aren't used to Jewish troubles, card players, flies, sickness, gullies and pits into which the unwary traveller could stumble.

'No swimming or climbing, or sleeping in gullies,' Klara warns Elya before he goes on the road. Sleeping in cemeteries is also forbidden. Entering cemeteries, Jewish or otherwise, after dark, when the dead walk and talk in high-pitched voices like young girls, is especially forbidden. Even passing a cemetery at night is forbidden.

'No taverns or taprooms, or talking to women.'

Elya almost laughs out loud. Doesn't he hear what his mother is saying? Apparently not. He knows what she's doing. Misunderstanding her son's intentions and extinguishing his dreams, what else is a mother for? He counts down the days. Three weeks until he's due to leave for Lublin. Three *farkakta* weeks.

Farkakta means shitty, if anyone's interested.

'You forgot drowning,' he says. 'Can't I drown?'

'You can, especially if you sleep in a gully and it starts to rain.'

She asks for a miracle that will transform her Elya back into a dutiful son, calling forth Jewish angels the size of cats with multi-coloured wings. She prays, fasts, sleeps on the floor as penance, recites psalms on her knees. To keep him at home, she sneaks in while Elya's sleeping and passes a handful of salt around his head, throwing a little in each corner, and over the threshold. 'Why Lublin?' she asks the cat. 'What's in Lublin?'

'I'll tell you what's in Lublin,' she answers before the cat even opens his mouth. 'Traffic, noise, filth, horse carcasses, women with cold eyes.' She kisses her son three times, spitting after each kiss to ward off the evil eye. She warns him that it is unlucky to dream of money.

Money, however, will enter his dreams.

He's got to go.

There are fifty-four streets in Mezritsh and Elya's bored of each one. Bored of the riverbank; the granary; the carts; the cart horses hanging their heads; the feedbags hanging from the heads of these horses; the little birds that peck the grain that falls from the feedbags that hang from the heads of these horses; the brick-yards; even the rope-twisting factory that interested him as a lad; the squabbling; the storytelling.

Klara pulls her own hair and beats her fists against the wall. She curses Kiva's uncle for supplying the goods to sell. She curses the journey, the road, her foolish son and his friends, their future wives and children, and their children's children. Later she'll regret this moment of madness. But a curse, once spoken, cannot be withdrawn. Words and eggs, as they say in Mezritsh, must be handled with care. Elya wants her approval, her blessing. A curse is what he gets instead.

'Promise you'll never sleep in a gully,' she cries.

What is it about gullies? He has no intention of sleeping in a gully, but it could happen. At the time, the thought of himself asleep in a ditch, having a laugh with Ziv and Kiva, excites him. 'I promise,' he lies. He's grown colder, more calculating of late. The more desperate she becomes, the easier it is to resist her.

'If you could go back home for five minutes,' Kiva, huddling on a ledge over the disappearing road to Lublin, is asking between sobs, 'what would you do?'

Hug Rifka, Elya thinks, hearing his sister pushing a broom up and down, slowly until spotted by Klara, then sweeping like the wind. Or maybe he's really hearing the wind, brushing wet leaves, wet twigs, and small wet branches across the wet forest floor. As if in a dream, he sees Rifka pick up Zusa, who is red-faced and squirming, too old to be carried. Who knew Zusa would grow up to be such a beauty? Blue-eyed, blonde and icy, like an American actress.

'I knew,' says Klara.

Zusa falls asleep in Rifka's arms. When she wakes they'll play a new game. Zusa must pretend to be a fire burning down the

Mezritsher shul, roaring and waving her little hands and fingers about like flames, while Rifka with a bucket of water pretends to put her out.

When the rain briefly eases, Elya, Kiva and Ziv try to regain the road, climbing a muddy embankment. Ziv, who has excellent balance, is in the lead, while Kiva, hanging on to Ziv's shirt tails, loses his footing and slides back down again. For a moment Elya, hugging their brush case, considers leaving him there. But Ziv climbs down and pulls Kiva to his feet. 'If we ever get out of here,' Kiva calls to Elya as he's helped to the top of the embankment by Ziv, 'promise me we'll just go home.'

'I promise,' says Elya.

Ziv, wearing his Russian novel open on his head like a hat, holds up Kiva, weeping and coughing. More mud swirls. More grass is flattened. More things fall from trees. Kiva sinks again. This time into a muddy puddle, deeper than it appears. And Ziv must rescue him again. Hoping not to die, Ziv, Elya and Kiva all promise their lives to Adoshem, although only one of them will keep his promise.

They trudge on. Then up ahead, as if by magic, a hostelry appears. A sign swinging high above the door depicts a steaming samovar and a red salami. Refuge! But even as Elya breaks into a run, the others following behind, he feels a warning. Then he feels nothing but relief. Planks laid across the mud lead to the front door. When they get closer they see a second sign, NO COUGHERS. They look at Kiva. Kiva looks at the ground. Coughs. Looks up at his friends. Smiles.

The innkeeper, a big man with hairy nostrils and bulging shoulders, like a giant in a fairy tale, welcomes them warmly. They will stay for a meal and hire a room for the night. It's raining harder than ever. What else can they do?

Deluxe or economy? Pillows are extra.

Elya opens the purse he carries and prises out a coin. On one side is the double-headed eagle and the legend 'BANK OF RUSSIA'. On the other, the numeral five sitting atop a vine. He is about to hand it over, but finds, for one embarrassing moment, that he cannot release it. When Elya asks for directions to Lublin, the giant scratches his head. 'But you are versts from there. Many versts.'

Luckily the others have not heard. They are already warming themselves in front of the fire in a room called 'the lounge'. When Elya joins them, they're introduced to the other honoured guests. A Barrel Seller from the north; a young man with a beard trimmed in the Russian style, who claims to be in timber; and an old man who's made a fortune in seeds and is looking for new investors. 'Vi getes?' the old man asks. He's wearing patent-leather shoes like a Lubliner; the Timber Trader, snub-toed boots; the Barrel Seller, ready-mades so poorly stitched they have come unstitched in the rain. A Painter of Horses paces behind them, anxious to be on the road again. His shoes are pointy Krakowers once worn by the Polish nobility, the long toes braced with whalebones.

Are they still making those? Elya briefly wonders.

Why should he care? He's done with shoes.

The Seed Merchant is a great talker who can also sing. The lads, however, are careful not to be unreserved with their fellow travellers and give false names. 'I'm Kiva,' Ziv says. 'I'm Elya,' Kiva says. 'And I'm Ziv,' says Elya.

No one has ever met a Mezritsher before.

A tame Jewish dog lies on the hearth. Everyone agrees that there are Jewish and gentile animals. All geese and chickens, for example, are Jewish. Some horses and cats, of course. The dog looks balefully at Elya and he is reminded of his father.

When the dog gets up, Kiva lays his prayer book, swollen and shapeless, on a chair in front of the fire. Can it be saved?

Vapours rise from Kiva's wet clothes as he stands watching the flames.

'How goes your journey?' Mister Timber asks.

'We were ill-received in Russian Town,' Ziv tells him. 'But we gave them what for.'

'Really? Such valiant boys.'

The Timber Trader laughs. Then the Seed Merchant joins in. Standing too close, both admire Kiva's gold watch which he takes out to wind, fitting a tiny key into the fusee.

'We're not really merchants. This is just a one-off,' Ziv explains. And Elya glares at him.

Kiva coughs gently. 'Shush,' he's told.

Soon they're joined by a Smoked Fish Broker wearing field shoes, who smiles, displaying a tooth edged with gold. 'What's this?' He picks up Kiva's drying prayer book, holds it between two fingers, then lets it drop.

'Don't mind him. He's an apostate,' the Seed Merchant whispers, and Elya stares at the man in wonder, having never met an apostate before. Ziv, meanwhile, selects a bawdy gentleman's magazine from a stack provided for the guests' entertainment, and begins to read. And Kiva? Eyes watering from no coughing, Kiva excuses himself.

'Cough, cough,' he says behind the door.

Elya also withdraws in order to open the brush case and check on their brushes. All are dry. Praise for moss litter, spongy, lightweight and brown in colour, gathered from the moors and bogs of north-east England and exported around the world.

XIX

Later, all seated at an enormous *tish*, they order from a menu that includes chicken broth with egg noodles or knaidlach, pancakes and liver, carrot pudding, raisin bread, and strudel, but choose, at Elya's insistence, only the cheapest roasted groats. And three glasses of tea. Wouldn't the young sirs like to see the drinks menu? No? The innkeeper, having put on a white jacket, is their server. He has a *monopolka*, an exclusive right to sell alcoholic beverages, and draws corks from the merchants' many bottles.

The merchants order meat with potato balls in rich gravy, a speciality of the region, carried in on a pillow.

When their own food arrives, Kiva gazes suspiciously at his plate.

'Who ordered the clean glass?' the innkeeper asks. He's heard the joke. Obviously. Everyone's heard that joke.

'What's this?' Kiva takes a cautious bite. 'Meat?'

'We didn't order meat,' Elya tells him.

The meat is salty and sweet, dark and deep.

'Sausage?' Ziv opines.

'Did we order sausage?' Kiva drops his cutlery.

Elya shakes his head. 'Too expensive.'

'They gave us sausage.'

'I think it's pork sausage,' Ziv winks at Elya.

'Pork!' Kiva retches. 'Sausage!'

'Only joking,' says Ziv. 'It's Jewish pork.'

'A *rabbi always wanted to try pork*,' says Elya. '*He drives his carriage one night to a distant Polish inn and orders this forbidden food. And plenty of it. Just as the waiter sets down a whole roast pig with an apple in its mouth, the door opens and a group of men from his synagogue enter. They stare at the rabbi in disbelief.*

"*What kind of* farkakta *inn is this?*" *the rabbi greets them, throwing up his hands.* "*You order an apple and this is how they serve it?*"'

The merchants laugh uproariously. And demand another, while Kiva toys with his meal. He will not be consoled. The innkeeper looks on disapprovingly. He resents this spoiled boy. He also resents the food he cooks, the small white jacket he wears, the swelling in his legs and ankles, his itchy skin, dark urine, and pale faeces. Soon he'll be dead from a fatty liver. Thereafter Kiva spends the evening throwing up. Food. Old schnapps. Bile.

Elya listens to the slack drip of water from the roof of the inn. The rain has stopped. He opens a shuttered window to look out. A kitchen child is pouring slops into a drainage ditch already over-flowing. Behind him is a yard piled high with suitcases left by visitors. Left how? Abandoned, forgotten, seized for non-payment?

The room they are sharing is narrow with a low ceiling, heavily beamed. The others go straight to bed. But Elya joins the merchants in the lounge.

Pouring Elya a glass of wine, the Barrel Seller, the Seed Merchant, the Timber Trader, the apostate Smoked Fish Broker and the Painter of Horses discuss business with him as if he were one of them. Mister Seed, who resembles the Uncle, is looking for a blind partner, so-called. He clasps Elya's shoulders, merchant to merchant. Everyone is going to get rich, he confides. It cannot fail.

'You can purchase a wagon with the profits,' he urges.

'Save your shoe leather,' adds Mister Barrel, encouraging Elya to invest.

'You're nothing without a carriage,' Mister Timber puts in.

Mister Fish and the Horse Painter nod enthusiastically.

'Shall we do business?' Mister Seed enquires.

Elya stares at their shoes. A small deposit will hold Elya's place. Still he hesitates. He's a cautious lad. He needs to sleep on it. He'll decide in the morning.

It's after midnight. The candles have all burned down to nubs but Elya can scarcely bring himself to leave the company of these honourable men.

'Once I was just like you,' Mister Seed says solemnly. He predicts Elya will go far. Finally someone is taking him seriously. Walking on air, Elya goes to bed. But he's not alone. As he mounts the stairs, he's followed by the apostate Mister Fish, who thrusts a shiny card into his hands, then disappears.

By the light of the candle nub he carries, Elya looks down at the card and sees a man with a beard and a halo. He is holding a Christian cross in one hand and something Elya cannot make out in the other. He squints but the light's too dim, the object too small. The patron saint of merchants, Elya assumes, traders, commercial travellers, businessmen, brokers and vendors. He puts it in his pocket.

The card actually depicts Saint Crispin, patron saint of *shusters*, holding a hammer. If he'd turned it around, Elya would have seen the saint's martyrdom. He's tied to a tree, along with his brother, Crispinian, while soldiers tear strips of *fleysh* from their naked backs. Later their bodies are thrown into a river, millstones around their necks.

Despite Ziv's snoring, Kiva's coughing and moaning, Elya sleeps heavily for the first time in days. Only once does he wake, hearing voices whispering outside their room and a creaking door.

'*Bed comfortable, but irritation proceeding from fleas,*' Elya writes in his notebook next morning.

Outside the sun is shining. But when they gather together their possessions, they find Kiva's gold watch is missing.

'It was that *gonif* with the Russian beard! Or that *schnorrer* with the goatee,' cries Ziv. 'Maybe it was the *shmuck* wearing patent-leather shoes,' adds Elya. 'Or the one with the snub-toed boots?'

'Most certainly it was the apostate Smoked Fish Broker,' says Kiva.

'Or all of them together,' concludes Elya.

Chokey, as if he's swallowed the point of a *shtek*, Elya feels a fool. Timber, seeds, barrels and smoked fish rain down on him as if from above. When they confront the innkeeper, they find that all the men have checked out. 'What do you want me to do,' the innkeeper grumbles, 'call the police?'

The police are more feared than Cossacks.

They're lucky to get away with the shoes on their feet. And the money belt around Elya's waist. Elya steals a plate from the inn and when they are out of sight, he sails it through the air.

It shatters against a tree.

This is more like something Ziv would do.

Does it make Elya feel better?

It does.

He imagines a plate that would never break. That could be thrown through the air again and again. What would such a plate be made of? He doesn't know. But children would love it.

'Homeward,' cries Kiva.

Kiva thinks they're going home.

They aren't.

Lublin may be far away, but with new directions from the innkeeper, they will continue on as if nothing's happened.

'You promised,' Kiva snivels. He's dragging one leg, coughing and tasting blood. Taut grin, shrunken eyes, dripping nose, Kiva must have a fever because everything seems very bright and far away. He cannot move his neck. Seriously. He opens his prayer book. Brittle curling pages float off on the merest breeze.

There are fallen branches on the road, fallen leaves, fallen nests, dirt, grit, mud of course. The ditches are full of rainwater. The sun turns hazy. A strange grey light. A sour smell. Alongside the road, the ground is soft, giving way beneath every step. They pass a foaming river, a drowned field. The air is thick as tannery glue and the temperature is rising. A tree struck by lightning still burns like a candle.

'Cough, cough,' says Kiva. His coughing brings up a quantity of phlegm from fawn to dead leaf, and from dead leaf to burnt cork in colour; the consistency from sappy to gluey, from quick-moving to sluggish. His lungs, like the soft mass obtained from breaking and grinding rags before they are made into paper, inflate and deflate with a wet sound. He coughs violently, then looks around surprised. His sneezes are growing louder too, more desperate, *pish* trickling down his leg. Elya and Ziv jump away. Kiva is hot. Cold. His liver hurts. Point to your liver, Kiva. They argue about where the liver is. Well, something hurts. He's told to keep it to himself. There isn't much anyone can do. 'But you promised.' Kiva falls to his knees crying and begging. 'Are we your enemies that you brought us here? Why bring us here?' he asks Elya.

'He needs a doctor,' says Ziv.

'A doctor? Is that a joke? Where are we going to find a doctor?' A doctor brings trouble, as Elya well knows.

'A woman brags about her son the doctor. "He's a genius," she tells her friend. "You must go see him."

"But there's nothing wrong with me," the friend replies.

"Don't worry. He'll find something."'

Elya strains his ears. Hears no laughter.

174

Taking small, flat steps, Kiva dawdles under the dripping trees. *Carry me*, he wants to cry. Wishing for a portable folding cot and canvas litter, he struggles on.

'Let's just be happy,' Elya tells him.

Wisps of blue smoke rise in the still air, slowly swirling around them as they draw close to a spot at the side of the road where travellers must have made a fire. But there is no fire. Nor the blackened remains of a fire. Elya kicks the grass.

'Like the netherworld,' Kiva opines.

Soon they come upon a small Jewish village. A poor shul and a studyhouse, a market with three stalls. That's all there is. From one of the stalls they purchase milk, hard grey bread.

'There may not be any fresh bread until Lublin. But then,' cries Elya, 'Lublin bread!'

Ziv glares at him.

Put a sock in it, Elya. Before Ziv chops you one.

Kiva is too ill to glare. He needs to sit down. He drops his knapsack, the water flask when it's passed to him.

They camp in a muddy field and eat bread boiled in milk, Ziv feeding Kiva like a baby. Panting rapidly, fighting for air, Kiva tries and fails to stand up again. 'Don't touch me,' he cries, growing suddenly limp. Lying flat on the ground and jerking from side to side, his arms and legs going in all directions. It's almost comical.

Kiva thrashes, then ceases thrashing. They hover over him. Is he dead? As if in the presence of a corpse, they bow their heads. Then he sits up. 'Adoshem,' he cries, another *pish* stain down his trousers. He looks around. Adoshem wielding a flaming sword appears before him, accompanied by a lion who holds aloft the sacred scrolls. Adoshem! At last! Hovering above the trees.

Speaking in a voice that seems to come from a barrel, Adoshem tells Kiva exactly what He wants him to do in exchange for His mercy. And Kiva, without question or hesitation, agrees.

They shake him. And holler his name. But Kiva is no longer sat in a muddy field. He's hiding in the cave of his own mind with one hundred true prophets; in the cleft of a rock, babbling about the firmament, Adoshem moving upon the waters. Birds escaped out of snares encircle Kiva's head. 'No sight is devoid of Him,' Kiva raves. Then everything goes quiet and Kiva sees Cossacks in the big Mezritsher shul. Is he *meshugeneh*? Shoes in the cooking pots. Eyeglasses in the gutters. 'Children,' he rants, 'smoked like cigarettes, sold for kopeks; used as pillows, hammers; the Head Rabbi wearing a crown of mud.'

It comes from not voiding, Elya thinks, these visions of Kiva's. Perhaps if he were to move his bowels.

'People falling down and dying in the New Cemetery,' Kiva cries.

He's totally lost it.

Earlier that summer, Elya and Klara go to the New Cemetery to see Usher. Hottest day of the year so far. Eight o'clock in the morning. Three weeks until he leaves for Lublin. Walking down Brisker Street, lined on either side with thickets bristling with thorns, Elya carries his hat. Already he's *shvitzing*. He drops back, letting his mother, in her darkest dress, walk ahead.

The New Cemetery, to Elya's relief, is deserted. Lately it's been busier than usual, as those departing for America come to be photographed grouped around a family headstone. No professional mourners at this hour either, falling on the graves of strangers, weeping and wailing for kopeks. Klara nudges him and Elya puts on his hat. They walk between the headstones, Klara in the lead. 'Look, there's Yetta Steckler,' she cries. 'And Yoshke, you remember Yoshke.' She greets the departed with little screams of delight. But when they reach their destination, her mood turns sour. 'Your father's stone looks smaller than the rest. Didn't we order large?'

Usher's headstone, which Klara kisses, is indeed modest, a simple slab compared to those adorned with carvings and lengthy epitaphs.

'Usher!' Klara gets down on her hands and knees and calls out his name.

'Can you get up?' Elya squirms with embarrassment beside her. He's not an unfeeling lad, he's agreed to accompany his mother in order to please her, but her sentiments bewilder and embarrass him. 'Can we go now?' He wills her to stand up and act normal.

'We just got here,' she says, sitting down and beckoning him to join her. His father's name, USHER GRYNBERG, is carved deeply into the granite at the top of his headstone, leaving room for the rest of the family.

The cemetery is like an oven. Elya recites Kaddish for his father, praising God and expressing a yearning for His kingdom on earth. '*Yisgadal, v'yiskadash smey rabba . . .*' and so forth.

Is it time for a joke?

'*A man visiting a cemetery notices another man kneeling beside a headstone. "Why did you have to die?" cries the kneeling man.*

"*Who are you mourning so passionately?" he's asked.*

"*My wife's first husband," he replies.*'

Elya's mother is stony-faced.

Well, what did he expect?

Three weeks, he thinks.

Elya remembers the joy of finally leaving Mezritsh. He's had his hair cut in a Polish style and Klara cries when she sees him. On a piece of paper, he writes the name 'Libka'. Then, before burying it deep inside his knapsack, he kisses it. And the prune pit? Shivering with delight, he puts it into his own mouth, then his pocket. Has he got everything? He shoulders past a basket suspended from the ceiling where baby Zusa once slept, now occupied by the cat. The cat, tipped out of the basket by Elya's careless shoulder, runs into the oven, still warm from the night before.

Elya hugs Zusa and Rifka. He opens the back door, ducks his head and steps quickly into the alleyway. Then, distracted by her son's departure, Klara lights the oven without first checking for the cat, who's consequently burned to a crisp, causing Klara, when she discovers her mistake, to weep all the tears she's stored up since forever.

If only there were ovens with glass doors.

This is the first of many forgetful accidents Klara will have in the years to come. In time, she'll forget the words and phrases she knows well, people's names, and the names of objects. She'll talk to the air and wander the streets, unable to find her way home.

In 1906, a neuropathologist and psychiatrist called Alois Alzheimer describes a peculiar disease of the cerebral cortex in a lecture to the 37th Conference of German Psychiatrists in Tübingen. Following this, he presents to the German Society of Alienists the results of an autopsy he's performed on the brain of such a patient, which shows two abnormalities, neurofibrillary tangles and amyloid plaques, also known as senile plaques.

Klara may already have these.

If not now. Coming soon.

Around their campsite, along the everlasting road to Lublin, dusk passes in the wink of an eye and then it's night. Elya lights a small fire. The damp wood pops and crackles, sending sparks up into the sky, then smoulders and dies.

'In *Herr Doktor*'s kitchen,' Elya tells Kiva and Ziv, 'there's a canister of gas hidden inside the stove. When his cook strikes a match and turns a knob, a flame appears on which you could fry an œuf.'

'What's an œuf?'

No one knows, not even Elya.

They laugh as if this is a joke. Finally, Elya has told another funny joke and for a moment time stands still. Then Ziv jumps up, Kiva falls down, and everything starts moving forward again and cannot be stopped. Without even a fire, it's so dark they can't tell a shovel from an axe; a worker's pamphlet from a prayer book; a prune pit from a purgative pill. Ziv lights a candle stolen from the inn. The flame flickers although there is no wind. Then Kiva's coughing again.

The sound puts Elya in mind of his father.

One unseasonably mild January, Elya's father leaves off his great-coat. Soon after he develops a cough, occasionally producing phlegm.

Before he takes to his bed, Usher reclines on a chair in the front room, a feather cushion behind his back. 'It's good to have a rest,' Usher tells Klara. '*Es iz gut.*' He rolls his large shoulders with pleasure, while Elya watches uneasily. His father has never stayed home from work before. Is it like a holiday? Elya doesn't think so. The cat dabs a paw into Usher's cold tea, after which, without willing it, Elya's father falls asleep.

When he wakes, his shirt front is speckled with blood. *Farsteysh?*

'No doctor,' he insists. But a doctor is called. Elya aged ten and Rifka aged seven cringe away, but his brother Fishel, nearly nine, creeps closer to have a look at the instruments in the doctor's case. Long, short and hooked knives, scalpels and needles. But where are the leeches?

No need to worry, the doctor reassures them. It's nothing a little rest won't cure. *Herr Doktor*, as he likes to be called, having studied medicine in Vienna, removes his pince-nez and, rubbing the reddened bridge of his nose, diagnoses a bacillus, an unwholesome agent invisible to the eye, seeping across the windowsills, through cracks in the walls and up between the floorboards.

'A *doctor comes to see his patient.*

"*I have some bad news and some very bad news.*"

"*You might as well give me the bad news first,*" *says his patient.*

"*You're very sick. In fact, you only have twenty-four hours to live.*"

"*Twenty-four hours! That's terrible! What's the very bad news?*"

"*I've been trying to reach you since yesterday.*"'

'Is it funny?' Elya enquires. And you must tell him it is.

Klara, wearing her best dress for *Herr Doktor*, shows him to the best chair and lets him sit. Usher will be dancing at Rifka's wedding, *Herr Doktor* promises with a wink, which is another way of saying he will not just live but thrive. Elya feels like dancing himself. Only the troubling thought that tall Rifka may never marry disturbs this hopeful moment. Then they all line up to shake the doctor's hand and wish him a good year, a prosperous year. Tears of gratitude in their eyes.

Never wish a doctor a prosperous year.

The next time he's called, *Herr Doktor* draws a quantity of blood from Usher's forearm using a spring-loaded lancet, but there's no improvement.

'Herr Doktor *gives a sick man five months to live, but he can't pay his bill, so* Herr Doktor *gives him five months more.*'

How will Klara pay the doctor? How will she dress poor Rifka to procure an advantageous marriage? Any marriage? She considers the butcher's wall-eyed apprentice. While she worries, the front room fills up with smoke. *Gevalt*! She's not been watching the cook stove. She hurries over and removes a pan of water that has boiled dry. 'Rifka!' she hollers. 'Rifka!' Whatever goes wrong, Rifka is always to blame. Meanwhile, in the narrow passageway outside Usher's room, the Angel of Death paces, his huge stiff wings scraping against the walls. It's said that if you watch a funeral procession through the eye of a needle you can see the Angel of Death with his sword, but you better not. Seriously, Elya is told. Don't!

XX

In the morning, on the never-ending road to Lublin, the sky turns white, then red. Kiva is weak but resolute. His eyes burn with intention and all the softness flows out of his face. 'He has to rest. He can't travel.' Ziv squats beside him, puts his arms around Kiva's shoulders and draws him close. '*Petseleh putz*,' he croons tenderly. He holds the cup while Kiva drinks.

Elya watching is surprised to see how large Kiva's eyes have become overnight. How small his body. Where's his *pupik*? And his sweet childish smile?

Ziv can whistle through a blade of grass and tries to show Kiva how. But Kiva remains elsewhere. What use has he for blades of grass or whistling now?

Elya paces. He cannot help it. Stay or go? His thoughts swing back and forth like a kerosene lamp dangling on a loose chain from some poor *shtetl* ceiling. 'Shall we start walking again?' he asks at last.

'Walking?' Ziv scowls.

'Yeah. Walking.'

'The only road that matters now is the road to Adoshem,' says Kiva. His child's face sharp. His clothes too big. Ziv wraps him tenderly in a blanket and strokes his *sheyna punim*. Elya wants to touch him too, to put out his hands and tell him everything will be all right, but something holds him back. 'I saw Adoshem,' Kiva jabbers. But how Kiva can see anything is a mystery. The lenses of his eyeglasses are covered in dirt, ash, sludge. 'Here, let me clean them for you,' says Ziv.

It is an effort for him to stand, but Kiva knows where he is going. Late in the afternoon, he leads Elya and Ziv back along the road, striding confidently, for Kiva, into the future. He doesn't need a hand, an elbow, or a stick to walk upright. Chest pushed out. Arms bouncing. It isn't far.

Where to?

The little Jewish village they passed yesterday and a studyhouse beside the shul.

Is Kiva sure?

He's sure.

Before entering, he washes his hands in a barrel of rainwater outside the door. Inside is a long table made of planks; the smell of old books; cobwebs; raw earth; a dark ceiling; sagging shelves. A holy book bound in wood lies open on the table. Men crowd around it.

The day has turned cool. A poor fire barely warms the room. Scholars with pale faces, like Kiva's face, wearing old-fashioned garments, hum and whisper, chanting and shivering as they pray. They take no interest in the world around them. 'What Tsar?' they ask, bemused. 'What drought?' 'What rain?' 'What kasha?'

The saltiest, plumpest kasha. How about it Kiva?

But Kiva's only interested in holy books now, praying and fasting. 'What more does a man need?' he will ask, his eyes bright with joy. 'A *shtikel brod*? A *sip fun wasser*?' He gives Ziv his shoes. He won't be requiring them any more. He trades his fine clothes for the tattered garments of a zealot, a true believer, a prophet. Kiva, with his soft shoulders, short arms, plump hands, irregular bowel movements, prune pastries and sweet kasha pudding, is abandoning the false distractions of life. Even the faces of his dear friends will soon be forgotten.

A small lamp burns throughout the night, while Elya and Ziv try to sleep on the crude studyhouse benches. In the morning, they shake hands solemnly. Kiva's grasp firmer than before.

Ziv's eyes are wet. And Elya? Poor Elya still believes this trip is a real trip. 'It's not real,' Kiva tells him.

Then Kiva returns to his prayers, his holy books, his *shtikel* bread. Sneer all you want, his eyes are radiating a strange, clear light. They must go on without him.

'I won't do it,' Ziv says.

'What'll I tell your mother?' Elya bleats.

Elya's last view of Kiva: sitting in the presence of the Holy Scrolls, wearing a long, tattered coat and a worn satin hat, and smiling.

'A *zay gezunt* Kiva.'

Elya and Ziv continue on their own without him. What else can they do? There's a greater sense of urgency now. Ziv can move fast when he wants to. Elya always wants to. They don't talk much. They just walk. After a while they come to a sign. LUBLIN. 100 VERSTS. Holy *drek*! They're further away than when they started. They've been walking in circles. And in the wrong direction. Can it be true? They examine the sign. A sign doesn't lie. It's far, but it's Lublin.

They're on the right path at last.

Elya doesn't just want to please the Uncle now. He wants to be the Uncle. Eventually he may come to resemble the Uncle, with a small paunch and skinny legs. In Lublin, he thinks, he'll buy Libka a ring.

Insects trail after them as they wander into a poor region of unpaved roads. No birdsong. Only the whirling of insect wings getting louder and louder. Or maybe it's the first aeroplane to fly over Poland. They look up. Cheer. At the sight of such a marvel, who could foresee anything but cheering? The light is bewildering, vexing, dreamlike as they blunder down the road. Then the sun comes out. They cross an iron bridge over a swollen river. Ziv looks back for Kiva. He isn't there.

'Remember Ahab,' says Ziv.

'Who?'

'One of the four wicked kings of Israel.'

'I think he made those stories up.'

'How did he die?' asks Ziv.

'Kiva's not dead!'

'Ahab.'

'A woman hit him over the head with a millstone.'

'That was Abimelech. I want to know about Ahab the idolator. How was he killed?'

'I can't remember. Why do you want to know?'

Ziv shrugs and they walk on.

Ahab died, Kiva would tell him, by an unaimed arrow, an accident, which Ziv would find disappointing.

The road ahead is trembling. First it only trembles a bit. Then a bit more. A ringing, grating, churning sound. A shrill whistle. Hoofbeats. Boots. Elya and Ziv dive into a ditch as a long column of mounted and unmounted Russian soldiers comes into view. They are hauling a large gun on a carriage. Ziv reaches for Elya's hand. First, they stare wide-eyed. Then, still holding hands, they stand up and cry, 'Hurrah!' They can't help themselves. They're just boys after all. And, well, it's affecting. They have seldom seen soldiers in Mezritsh, although one day the town will be occupied by them, commandeered by a general, if you can believe that. And no one can. But never mind. It's all in the future, a million versts away.

Ziv drops Elya's hand. 'Get off,' he says.

When they regain the road, a carriage bus overtakes them, scattering road grit, the passengers laughing, eating, waving and shouting.

Ziv keeps looking back. Kiva still isn't coming.

There are half-burned trees everywhere. A dead *gonif* swings from a rope tied to a low branch. He's been there a while.

'Imagine if Kiva was here?' Ziv's eyes twitch up to the branch and away. Wearing Kiva's superior shoes, he lifts his feet high as if stepping, like Kiva, over something unpleasant. And he is: animal excrement; small corpses; rotting vegetation.

They pass no villages and find nothing to eat. One night they try to make soup from sorrel leaves. Elya's mother makes this soup, which is Elya's favourite, with one quarter of a pound of sorrel, six cups of water, one teaspoon of paprika and three beaten eggs. She serves it with sour cream and more eggs, hard-boiled.

The soup they make has no eggs, no sour cream, no paprika.

'I can't taste anything,' Ziv complains.

'You're lucky.'

Oh, for a cup of tea.

But there's no tea either. Not even in Mezritsh, where tea has lately become scarce. The only tea you can buy tastes like kerosene. Kerosene is also in short supply. A shipment, anxiously expected, mysteriously ignites and an enormous ball of flame pitches down the Mezritsh highway towards Biale, narrowly missing two *Khappers* and a line of boys they have captured.

Another night Elya and Ziv eat road seeds and unripe berries from a thorny bush. They pick bad mushrooms. Well, they looked all right. Then they're sick. Next day, too weak to walk further, they locate a carriage stop in a posting yard outside an inn and hire two places on a goods wagon to Lublin. The night wagon is a poor one with no kerosene headlamps to show the way. They're the only passengers, squeezed between a backload of barrels. They jolt over ruts in the road and groan. The inferior wheels are high and loose with large axles. Not a wagon that advertises a smooth ride. An uncovered economy wagon. The vehicle sways from side to side. They take the bends swiftly, the driver at first alert, wild whinnying from his lively horse. Eventually they all fall asleep. Including the driver. Perhaps he's been drinking. Swaying, he rouses himself, cursing the moon which drifts behind a bank of clouds; the dark, wet road; his ungrateful wife; his children. All he has is his horse. The horse throws back its head and snorts. Only good thing in his life, a horse. It's so dark he cannot see the road ahead. Then, skittering sideways on wet leaves, his horse stumbles. The carriage lurches forward. Hits a tree and rolls into a ditch. Elya falls out, flung onto the road. Ziv falls on top of him. Broken barrels, upturned sacks, spilled grain.

Elya has a cut on his cheek. Ziv is out cold.

'Ziv, can you hear me?'

Ziv moans. Sits up.

They are stunned. Nearly dead. Seeing black spots before their eyes. Seeing birds, stars.

The driver also rouses himself. Face dark with blood, he stumbles. Finds his feet. Kicks the broken carriage wheels. His horse lies on its side, quivering, one eye rolling. The driver kneels close to the animal, then looks up and motions down the road. There's a village not far away, he tells them, and Elya and Ziv start walking.

Then Elya stops. The brushes! He runs back. Their beautiful brush case is dented and scratched. But when he opens it, he finds their brushes unharmed.

'No refunds!' the driver shouts after them.

After walking all night and most of the following day, they come upon the village promised by the driver. Not far, as it turns out, is far enough. The village as a destination is a disappointment. Polish peasants, barbed wire, crying children, starving dogs, wooden huts with straw roofs or no roofs, goats; the roadside lined with gullies and deep ravines; more insects overhead, flying lower, buzzing louder; dusk falling from the trees. They ought to have hurried away. But it's getting dark and they decide to camp nearby.

That night, Ziv's restless. Looking into the shard of his mirror, he combs his hair. He's noticed a taproom. A what? A drinking establishment. Where? In the village. Trust Ziv. You couldn't miss it. Well, Ziv couldn't. How about it? A glass or two of schnapps? And Elya agrees. After all they've been through. Putting on his own fancy but ruined shoes, and throwing the stout footwear he received from Kiva in his knapsack, Ziv's ready. Elya changes his shirt. He tries to brush the mud off his knees.

A fearful place it looks at first. Never mind that. Ziv hurries towards the tavern door where men cluster. Soon they'll be beating each other senseless. This is what Ziv's been waiting for. But it's early yet. A drunk *pishes* against a wall. Elya stares in wonder at his long *putz* and uncircumcised foreskin. The front door opens. Closes. Opens. Crude tables. A dirt floor. Flies. There's some muttering as they enter. Are they not welcome? Nah, they're welcome. Peasants in blunt-toed boots wave their arms and shout.

'Good fellows,' Ziv opines, then he laughs. There are card players and dicers at the tables, cracking nuts and spitting shells; serious drinkers at the bar downing shots. And there are women, wagon girls like the women of Babylon. Ziv throbs with excitement. And Elya? Perhaps he throbs too.

They get drinks. Sit down. Immediately, they are joined by two thick-legged, beautiful women. Both called Magda. The Magda beside Elya grabs his ears and holds them tightly between her fingers and thumbs, twisting and laughing. 'What big ears you have,' she cries in Polish, and the nape of his neck flushes pink.

Ziv winks at him. 'Women,' he says.

'Women,' Elya nods. His mind, like Ziv's mind, confused by impure thoughts. Suddenly he feels handsome. 'Another drink?'

Ziv leans forward and reaches into Elya's money belt. And Elya lets him. He's not stupid. He's left most of their money at their campsite, buried underneath a tree. He knows which one. The brush case under a fall of leaves.

XXI

They raise a glass to absent Kiva. 'Remember his prayer face?'

'To Kiva!'

'Kiva!'

'To Lublin.'

'Lublin!'

Ziv downs his drink and orders another. 'This should be illegal,' he cries loud enough to wake Adoshem. Then he leans in closer. 'My mother beats me,' he confesses in a low voice.

'Your mother?'

'Who else?'

'But she's your mother.'

Ziv kisses the girl sat beside him. 'How about a *vitz*?' he asks Elya.

'You want a joke?'

'If you don't mind.' Ziv nudges his Magda. 'Listen up,' he says.

'A genie gives a drunk three wishes. The drunk doesn't even have to think about it. First, he wants a bottle that never empties. The genie waves his magic shtek, *and poof, a bottle of schnapps that never empties appears. The drunk drinks it right down and it fills up again. Then the genie says, "You've got two more wishes. So what'll it be?"*

"I'll have another one of these," slurs the drunk. "No wait, make it two."'

Both beautiful Magdas laugh, but their eyes wander. They don't understand a word of Yiddish. And Ziv? Ziv would laugh at anything tonight. 'The storm,' he cries out with joy. 'The storm's about to break!' His eyes sparkle with an appetite for life. He pounds Elya on the back, then gets up to dance, whirling and leaping, and spilling another man's drink. The man glares at him. And Ziv tries to apologise. A shifty Ziv apology. The man glares harder. A red face. Hair cropped to stubble.

'Go on, Jacek,' someone in a wolfskin cap cries out.

Jacek glares harder. Is that all he's going to do? Ziv's getting impatient. He curls up a fist.

'Take it outside,' the barman hollers.

'Gladly,' says Ziv. He snaps his big teeth in anticipation. Then he turns to Elya and grins. Elya tries to clear his head. He doesn't know what to do. 'Sit down, please,' he says to Ziv at last, tugging at Ziv's sleeve.

'*Gai plotz,*' responds Ziv with a laugh. He can take care of himself.

'I'm coming with you.'

'Don't bother. I'll be right back.'

Ziv turns away.

'Ziv?'

He's walking.

'Ziv?'

Still walking.

'Ziv?'

He's at the door.

'Ziv?'

He opens the door.

Then darkness swallows him up.

Ziv and the stubble-haired Jacek are followed out by more stubble-haired drinkers. And the Magda Ziv's been sitting next to. And the Magda Elya's been sitting next to. Pushing out, they leave the door open. Someone inside closes it again. Elya finishes his drink alone. Alone he waits for Ziv.

What's taking so long?

A tap on his shoulder. Elya turns around.

Libka!

Not Libka. A girl who looks just like her. Libka with an upturned nose. A sweet piggy face. She says her name's Magda.

How many Magdas are there?

Many.

Meanwhile, outside, Ziv's fighting. His lip is split, but he's smiling. His timing's off but he's happy. He's out of practice yet unburdened, stunned with relief. Around him, a crowd gathers. He's down. Then up. Puffing into his hands, he throws a punch. It lands. He throws another. Misses. Takes one to the jaw. Then flat on the ground again beside an open drain, tasting blood. Yes! he thinks. Grunting, he tries to get up. Up again, but buckling at the knees, punching the air. Down again, protecting his face with an elbow. Jacek accepting slaps on the back from his friends. 'Finish him off,' someone cries cheerfully. Girls in the alleyway run over to see. 'He spilled a drink,' they're told. 'On Jacek's shoes!'

The crowd presses closer. Up again. Down again. Swallowing a tooth. Is this what Ziv hoped for?

It is.

Then the Magda that Ziv flirted with, nudged, nuzzled, and bought a drink for, throws a stone at him. It lands on his head, disordering something in his brain. She looks around for another. Or an empty bottle. Once he's down, really down, she aims a little kick at his mouth. 'Don't stop now,' she eggs the others on. They're going to send Ziv up the chimney.

Which means what exactly?

It must mean something.

Well they aren't going to burn him, are they? Rough him up is all. Teach him a lesson he'll never forget.

*

'*Ikh heys Elya*,' Elya says inside the tavern to the girl beside him. '*Vi heystu?*'

She doesn't reply. Then he remembers. She's already told him her name's Magda. He raises his glass. Drinks. Smiles at the girl who smiles back at him.

'Where are you travelling to?' she asks.

At least he thinks that's what she asks.

'Lublin,' he says. 'Is it far?'

'Not far at all.'

Meanwhile, someone in the crowd of drinking men with thick legs and large hands, glares at Elya. '*Zydzi*,' he mutters.

Zydzi is a word Elya would comprehend, if Elya were listening, if his ears were sharper, if his attention were not entirely on the girl. Someone starts to sing. Stops. Starts again. The girl beside him says she can sing too. After the singing, more drinking. Then more muttering, dark looks in Elya's direction and a scraping back of chairs.

'Let's go,' the girl says suddenly. But Elya wants to stay. Stay and wait for Ziv. 'Who, him?' She screws up her pretty face. 'He's not coming back.'

'Isn't he?' Elya stares stupidly at the door. He labours to stand. 'Come on,' his Magda urges. She pulls. He follows. Out the back way.

Peering into a haze of darkness behind the tavern, Elya shakes his head. He doesn't understand that she's just saved him. In the distance, there's cheering. The sound of breaking glass.

How do we look together, Elya wonders drunkenly, as they race along a dark path lined with trees. Then off the path into a dense forest. More trees above. Rough earth below. Where are we going? he wants to ask, but his Polish isn't good enough. A wind rushes over the branches. A wind that is not cooling. She walks ahead now and he follows, waving his arms in the air and laughing. He cannot help himself. He forgets everything but her legs glimpsed through the thin material of her dress. Polish Libka, as he thinks of her. Not lithe as a lily, which is the finest artist's brush available. Sturdier. Her shoulders wide. Her gait confident. Arms long and strong. Hair pale and smooth, lying close to her head. 'Bad-luck boy,' she calls him. Or maybe he's misunderstood. He pushes closer. Polish is a beautiful language. He knows a bit. A *bisele*. Not enough.

'*Ver biztu?*' he says. And now she shrugs. Opens her mouth. Smiles wickedly. Dark gaps between her teeth. And Elya feels suddenly afraid. What's wrong with him? Confusing girls with brushes? Magdas with Libkas? What does he know about this girl? This Magda? Probably a wagon girl. No, certainly. Or a foul imp sent by a demon. He should leave, but how will he find his way back? Find the campsite? Find Ziv?

Forget all that. Just run. Run, he tells himself. But he doesn't run. He wants this girl and he can have her. Even when she stops to relieve herself behind a bush, he waits indulgently. He thinks evil cannot touch him. He thinks bad spirits cannot touch him.

Then she takes his arm. And they hurry on.

At last they enter the small wooden hut she says is home. It's dark inside. Darker than outside. A sour cabbage smell. Never mind. She speaks to him earnestly, putting a finger to her lips.

'*Ikh farshtey nisht*,' he tells her.

She doesn't understand him either. She kicks off her shoes, motions for him to do the same, then leads him to her unmade bed. A gritty sheet. But who's complaining? He thinks for one terrible moment of his mother and Rifka making the beds at home, shaking the *ibediks* until the feathers fly.

Magda knows what to do. She holds him firmly. Don't stop now, Elya moans. His knees tremble and his throat contracts. He wants to die in her arms.

*

In the night Elya wakes. Someone is breathing heavily nearby. Lifting himself on his elbows, he looks around. 'Who's that?' he asks the girl lying beside him.

'Only chickens and frogs,' she says. Even if he understood, he wouldn't understand. 'Go back to sleep.' She tucks the blanket around them.

'*Ikh ken nisht shlofen.*' He sits up. Sees for the first time another bed beside their bed. In this bed, there is a man asleep in a wolfskin cap. Her father? Brother? Husband? Elya fumbles for his trousers. Lifts his shoes. Tries to sneak to the door. Stumbles, rousing Magda who sits up and lights a candle. Looking sorrowfully at him, she holds out a hand.

What does she want?

Gelt.

The man in the next bed turns over.

Standing at the doorway, Elya empties his pockets. He has nothing but the silver coin given to him by his mother. And she takes it. Gladly.

From the cottage, Elya can see the road. It is not as far as it seemed last night. The forest not as dense, or dark. And he starts to walk.

Ziv, *may he hang upside down from a tree*, is not at their campsite. Where could he be? His bedroll is where he dropped it. Still rolled. Perhaps he's coming soon. Elya waits, mist rising around him like steam from a kettle. A dull morning.

When Ziv doesn't come, Elya digs up the money and retrieves the brush case he's hidden, hefts his own and Ziv's bedrolls and backpacks and goes to look for him. First he staggers to the tavern. The door's locked. The shutters down. He peers between the slats. Tables overturned. Glass on the floor. The alleyway is empty. The backyard is empty. 'Ziv,' he calls.

He's not worried. Ziv is somewhere sleeping it off. But where?

A small deserted marketplace? Ziv's not there selling brushes. A dump of rubbish? Ziv's not there hiding behind a pile of fish heads and broken boxes. On the road to Lublin? Ziv's not walking.

Elya searches everywhere. A child tethering a goat to a tree looks up. 'Have you seen my friend?' Elya asks in bad Polish. The child and his goat run away.

'Ziv?' Elya walks the village roads, calling.

It's a miracle he finds him. He's asleep in a ditch. 'Get up Ziv,' Elya hisses, jumping in beside him. No reply, which is just like Ziv. A gentle kick. And then another. 'I've been looking everywhere for you. How was I supposed to find you here? Why didn't you go back to the campsite? Huh? Ziv?'

Ziv is wearing a burlap bag over his head. His body is strangely twisted. Or is he just pretending? 'Take that off, you look stupid. Ziv! Ziv! Answer me!'

'Go whistle,' Ziv sits up and says.

Except he doesn't.

Later they will laugh about it. Ziv's arm in a sling. Later when they're walking towards Lublin again. Meanwhile Elya frets. 'Get up!' He glares at Ziv. A rope has been fastened around Ziv's neck. There's a name for a rope tied like that. Ziv's coat is ripped. One terrible cheap shoe is missing. Elya tries to straighten Ziv's legs. 'Help me,' he says to no one.

Maybe it isn't even Ziv.

'Ziv? *Vas mahkhsta?*'

Elya loosens the rope, then tenderly removes the burlap bag from Ziv's head.

Ziv's blue face is hardly a face at all. His teeth are broken. His chin collapsed. He was going to Lublin to bring home a beard. A false beard attached with spirit gum, if need be. He wasn't returning without one. He'd hate his mirror if he could see his face now.

There's a gash on Ziv's forehead. Bottle glass in his hair. What will Elya tell Ziv's mother, bent over her vat of hospital soup? He holds Ziv in an awkward embrace, eyes welling. There's blood on Elya's hands now. He wipes them on his trousers.

Moments later, he's running down the road. Running and crying. He runs a long time without stopping. Then Elya slows down. Stops. Takes out his map. Studies it. The sky overhead has a white appearance. The foliage is denser, the bushes taller. Fields on either side extend as far as the eye can see. He struggles with all the bags he carries but he's determined. The further he walks, the more determined he is. No one detains him now, or slows his pace. Moving quickly, he grows smaller and smaller, then the road curves, and Elya Grynberg vanishes forever behind a clump of trees.

ACKNOWLEDGEMENTS

My heartfelt thanks to the many, many friends and colleagues, too many to name, who have believed in me and encouraged my writing over the years. Also, great thanks to Tara Tobler whose sensitive editing and great respect for the writer and the writer's words infused the whole editing process with resourcefulness and joy. Finally, to Derek whose enduring love and support empowers me.

Dear readers,

As well as relying on bookshop sales, And Other Stories relies on subscriptions from people like you for many of our books, whose stories other publishers often consider too risky to take on.

Our subscribers don't just make the books physically happen. They also help us approach booksellers, because we can demonstrate that our books already have readers and fans. And they give us the security to publish in line with our values, which are collaborative, imaginative and 'shamelessly literary'.

All of our subscribers:

- receive a first-edition copy of each of the books they subscribe to
- are thanked by name at the end of our subscriber-supported books
- receive little extras from us by way of thank you, for example: postcards created by our authors

BECOME A SUBSCRIBER,
OR GIVE A SUBSCRIPTION TO A FRIEND

Visit andotherstories.org/subscriptions to help make our books happen. You can subscribe to books we're in the process of making. To purchase books we have already published, we urge you to support your local or favourite bookshop and order directly from them – the often unsung heroes of publishing.

OTHER WAYS TO GET INVOLVED

If you'd like to know about upcoming events and reading groups (our foreign-language reading groups help us choose books to publish, for example) you can:

- join our mailing list at: andotherstories.org
- follow us on Twitter: @andothertweets
- join us on Facebook: facebook.com/AndOtherStoriesBooks
- admire our books on Instagram: @andotherpics
- follow our blog: andotherstories.org/ampersand

THIS BOOK WAS MADE POSSIBLE
THANKS TO THE SUPPORT OF

Aaron McEnery
Aaron Schneider
Abigail Walton
Ada Gokay
Adam Lenson
Adriel Levine
Ajay Sharma
Al Ullman
Alan Hunter
Alan McMonagle
Alasdair Cross
Albert Puente
Alex Ramsey
Alexandra Stewart
Alexandra Webb
Ali Riley
Ali Smith
Ali Usman
Alice Clarke
Alice Wilkinson
Aliya Rashid
Allan & Mo Tennant
Alyssa Rinaldi
Alyssa Tauber
Amanda
Amado Floresca
Amaia Gabantxo
Amanda Astley
Amanda Dalton
Amber Da
Amelia Dowe
Amine Hamadache
Amitav Hajra
Amos Hintermann
Amy and Jamie
Amy Hatch
Amy Lloyd
Amy Sousa
Amy Tabb
Ana Novak
Andrea Barlien
Andrea Larsen
Andrea Oyarzabal Koppes

Andreas Zbinden
Andrew Burns
Andrew Kerr-Jarrett
Andrew Marston
Andrew Martino
Andrew McCallum
Andrew Place
Andrew Place
Andrew Rego
Andrew Wright
Andrzej Walzchojnacki
Andy Marshall
Ann Rees
Anna Finneran
Anna French
Anna Gibson
Anna Hawthorne
Anna Holmes
Anna Kornilova
Anna Milsom
Anna Zaranko
Anna-Maria Aurich
Anne Edyvean
Anne Frost
Anne Germanacos
Anne-Marie Renshaw
Anne Willborn
Anonymous
Ant Cotton
Anthony Cotton
Anthony Fortenberry
Anthony Quinn
Antonia Saske
Antony Pearce
April Hernandez
Archie Davies
Aron Trauring
Asako Serizawa
Ashleigh Sutton
Audrey Holmes
Audrey Small
Barbara Mellor
Barbara Spicer

Barry John Fletcher
Barry Norton
Becky Matthewson
Ben Buchwald
Ben Schofield
Ben Thornton
Ben Walter
Benjamin Judge
Benjamin Pester
Beth Heim de Bera
Beverley Thomas
Bill Fletcher
Billy-Ray Belcourt
Birgitta Karlén
Bjørnar Djupevik Hagen
Blazej Jedras
Brandon Clar
Brenda Wrobel
Brendan Dunne
Briallen Hopper
Brian Anderson
Brian Byrne
Brian Callaghan
Brian Isabelle
Brian Smith
Briana Sprague
Bridget Prentice
Brittany Redgate
Brooke Williams
Brooks Williams
Buck Johnston & Camp
   Bosworth
Burkhard Fehsenfeld
Buzz Poole
Caitlin Farr Hurst
Caitlin Halpern
Callie Steven
Cam Scott
Cameron Adams
Camilla Imperiali
Carl Emery
Carla Castanos
Carole Burns

Carole Parkhouse
Carolina Pineiro
Caroline Kim
Caroline Montanari
Caroline Musgrove
Caroline West
Carolyn Carter
Carolyn A Schroeder
Catharine Braithwaite
Catherine Jacobs
Catherine Lambert
Catherine Tandy
Catherine Williamson
Cathryn Siegal-Bergman
Cecilia Rossi
Cecilia Uribe
Cerileigh Guichelaar
Chandler Sanchez
Charles Dee Mitchell
Charles Fernyhough
Charles Heiner
Charles Kovach
Charles Rowe
Charlie Small
Charlotte Middleton
Charlotte Ryland
Charlotte Whittle
China Miéville
Chris Burton
Chris Clamp
Chris Johnstone
Chris McCann
Chris Potts
Chris Senior
Chris Stergalas
Chris Stevenson
Christian Schuhmann
Christina Sarver
Christine Bartels
Christine Elliott
Christopher Fox
Christopher Stout
Ciara Callaghan
Claire Mackintosh
Claire Riley
Claire Williams
Clare Wilkins

Claudia Mazzoncini
Cliona Quigley
Colin Denyer
Colin Hewlett
Colin Matthews
Collin Brooke
Conor McMeel
Courtney Daniel
Courtney Lilly
Craig Kennedy
Cynthia De La Torre
Cyrus Massoudi
Daisy Savage
Dale Wisely
Damon Copeland
Daniel Cossai
Daniel Gillespie
Daniel Hahn
Daniel Jones
Daniel Sanford
Daniel Syrovy
Daniela Steierberg
Darcie Vigliano
Darren Boyling
Darren Gillen
Darryll Rogers
Darya Lisouskaya
Dave Lander
David Alderson
David Anderson
David Ball
David Eales
David Greenlaw
David Gunnarsson
David Hebblethwaite
David Higgins
David Johnson-Davies
David Kaus
David F Long
David Miller
David Richardson
David Shriver
David Smith
David Smith
David Wacks
Davis MacMillan
Dawn Bass

Dawn Walter
Dean Taucher
Debbie Pinfold
Deborah Green
Deborah McLean
Declan O'Driscoll
Denis Larose
Denis Stillewagt & Anca
  Fronescu
Denise Brown
Diane Hamilton
Diane Josefowicz
Dietrich Menzel
Dominic Bailey
Dominic Nolan
Dominick Santa Cattarina
Dominique Brocard
Dominique Hudson
Doris Duhennois
Douglas Smoot
Dugald Mackie
Duncan Chambers
Duncan Clubb
Duncan Macgregor
Dustin Chase-Woods
Dyanne Prinsen
E Rodgers
Earl James
Ebba Tornérhielm
Ed Smith
Edward Champion
Ekaterina Beliakova
Eleanor Maier
Elif Aganoglu
Elina Zicmane
Elizabeth Atkinson
Elizabeth Balmain
Elizabeth Braswell
Elizabeth Cochrane
Elizabeth Coombes
Elizabeth Draper
Elizabeth Franz
Elizabeth Leach
Elizabeth Rice
Elizabeth Seals
Elizabeth Sieminski
Ella Sabiduria

Ellen Agnew
Ellen Beardsworth
Emiliano Gomez
Emily Gladhart
Emily Walker
Emma Barraclough
Emma Bielecki
Emma Coulson
Emma Louise Grove
Emma Post
Emma Teale
Eric Anderson
Erin Cameron Allen
Erin Feeley
Ethan White
Evelyn Reis
Ewan Tant
Fay Barrett
Faye Williams
Felicity Le Quesne
Felix Valdivieso
Finbarr Farragher
Fiona Liddle
Fiona Quinn
Fiona Wilson
Fran Sanderson
Frances Dinger
Frances Harvey
Francesca Brooks
Francesca Rhydderch
Frank Pearson
Frank Rodrigues
Frank van Orsouw
Gabriel Garcia
Gabriella Roncone
Gavin Aitchison
Gawain Espley
Gemma Alexander
Gemma Bird
Gemma Hopkins
Geoff Thrower
Geoffrey Cohen
Geoffrey Urland
George McCaig
George Stanbury
George Wilkinson
Georgia Panteli

Georgia Shomidie
Georgina Hildick-Smith
Georgina Norton
Gerry Craddock
Gill Boag-Munroe
Gillian Grant
Gillian Spencer
Gillian Stern
Gina Filo
Gina Heathcote
Glen Bornais
Glenn Russell
Gloria Gunn
Gordon Cameron
Gosia Pennar
Graham Blenkinsop
Graham R Foster
Grainne Otoole
Grant Ray-Howett
Hadil Balzan
Halina Schiffman-Shilo
Hannah Freeman
Hannah Rapley
Hannah Vidmark
Hannah Jane Lownsbrough
Hans Lazda
Harriet Stiles
Haydon Spenceley
Heidi Gilhooly
Helen Alexander
Helen Berry
Helen Mort
Henrike Laehnemann
Holly Down
Howard Robinson
Hyoung-Won Park
Ian Betteridge
Ian McMillan
Ian Mond
Ida Grochowska
Ilya Markov
Imogen Clarke
Ines Alfano
Inga Gaile
Irene Mansfield
Irina Tzanova
Isabella Livorni

Isabella Weibrecht
J Drew Hancock-Teed
Jack Brown
Jacob Musser
Jacqueline Lademann
Jacqueline Vint
Jake Baldwinson
Jake Newby
James Attlee
James Avery
James Beck
James Crossley
James Cubbon
James Leonard
James Portlock
James Richards
James Ruland
James Scudamore
James Ward
James Higgs
Jamie Mollart
Jamie Veitch
Jan Hicks
Jane Bryce
Jane Dolman
Jane Leuchter
Jane Roberts
Jane Roberts
Jane Woollard
Janet Digby
Janis Carpenter
Jason Bell
Jason Montano
Jason Timermanis
JE Crispin
Jeff Collins
Jeff Fesperman
Jeffrey Davies
Jen Hardwicke
Jenifer Logie
Jennifer Fain
Jennifer Fosket
Jennifer Frost
Jennifer Harvey
Jennifer Mills
Jennifer Watts
Jennifer Yanoschak

Jenny Huth
Jenny McNally
Jeremy Koenig
Jeremy Morton
Jeremy Sabol
Jerome Mersky
Jerry Simcock
Jess Decamps
Jess Wood
Jesse Coleman
Jessica Kibler
Jessica Queree
Jessica Weetch
Jethro Soutar
Jill Harrison
Jo Lateu
Joanna Luloff
Joanna Trachtenberg
Joao Pedro Bragatti
  Winckler
JoDee Brandon
Jodie Adams
Joe Huggins
Joel Hulseman
Joel Swerdlow
Johannes Holmqvist
Johannes Menzel
John Berube
John Bogg
John Carnahan
John Conway
John Gent
John Hodgson
John Kelly
John Miller
John Purser
John Reid
John Shaw
John Steigerwald
John Walsh
John Whiteside
John Winkelman
Jolene Smith
Jon Riches
Jonathan Blaney
Jonathan Harris
Jonathan Huston

Jonathan Woollen
Joni Chan
Jonny Anderson
Jonny Kiehlmann
Jordana Carlin
Joseph Darlington
Josephine Glöckner
Josh Glitz
Josh Sumner
Joshua Briggs
Joshua Davis
Joy Paul
Judith Gruet-Kaye
Julia Von Dem Knesebeck
Julie Atherton
Julie Greenwalt
Juliet Swann
Junius Hoffman
Jupiter Jones
Juraj Janik
Justine Sherwood
Kaarina Hollo
Kalina Rose
Kamaryn Norris
Karen Gilbert
Karen Mahinski
Katarzyna Bartoszynska
Kate Beswick
Kate Carlton-Reditt
Kate Rizzo
Katharine Robbins
Kathryn Edwards
Kathryn Williams
Kati Hallikainen
Katie Brown
Katie Cooke
Katie Freeman
Katie Grant
Katrina Mayson
Katy Robinson
Kavitha Buggana
Keith Walker
Kelly Hydrick
Kelsey Grashoff
Kenneth Blythe
Kent McKernan
Kerry Broderick

Kerry Parke
Kieran Rollin
Kieron James
Kris Ann Trimis
Kristen Tcherneshoff
Kristen Tracey
Kristin Djuve
Kristy Richardson
Krystale Tremblay-Moll
Krystine Phelps
Kurt Navratil
Kyle Pienaar
Kyra Wilder
Lana Selby
Laura Ling
Laura Murphy
Laura Rangeley
Lauren Pout
Lauren Schluneger
Lauren Trestler
Laurence Laluyaux
Leah Binns
Lee Harbour
Leelynn Brady
Leona Iosifidou
Lex Orgera
Liliana Lobato
Lilie Weaver
Lily Blacksell
Linda Jones
Linda Whittle
Lindsay Attree
Lindsay Brammer
Lindsey Ford
Lisa Simpson
Liz Clifford
Liz Ketch
Liz Ladd
Lorna Bleach
Louise Aitken
Louise Evans
Louise Jolliffe
Lucinda Smith
Lucy Moffatt
Luiz Cesar Peres
Luke Murphy
Lydia Syson

Lynda Graham
Lyndia Thomas
Lynn Fung
Lynn Grant
Lynn Martin
Madalyn Marcus
Maeve Lambe
Malgorzata Rokicka
Mandy Wight
Marco Medjimorec
Margaret Jull Costa
Mari-Liis Calloway
Maria Lomunno
María Losada
Marie Cloutier
Marijana Rimac
Marina Castledine
Marina Jones
Marion Pennicuik
Mark Grainger
Mark Reynolds
Mark Sargent
Mark Sheets
Mark Sztyber
Mark Tronco
Mark Troop
Mark Waters
Martin Nathan
Mary Addonizio
Mary Clarke
Mary Heiss
Mary Tinebinal
Mary Wang
Maryse Meijer
Mathias Ruthner
Mathilde Pascal
Matt Davies
Matthew Cooke
Matthew Crossan
Matthew Eatough
Matthew Francis
Matthew Gill
Matthew Lowe
Matthew Woodman
Matthias Rosenberg
Max Longman
Maxwell Mankoff

Maya Feile Tomes
Meaghan Delahunt
Meg Lovelock
Megan Wittling
Mel Pryor
Michael Bichko
Michael Bittner
Michael Boog
Michael Eades
Michael James Eastwood
Michael Floyd
Michael Gavin
Michael Parsons
Michael Schneiderman
Michele Whitfeld
Michelle Mercaldo
Michelle Mirabella
Miguel Head
Mike Abram
Mike James
Mike Schneider
Miles Smith-Morris
Mim Lucy
Miranda Gold
Mohamed Tonsy
Molly Foster
Monica Tanouye
Morgan Lyons
Moriah Haefner
Nancy Chen
Nancy Jacobson
Nancy Oakes
Nancy Peters
Naomi Morauf
Nasiera Foflonker
Nathalia Robbins-Cherry
Nathalie Teitler
Nathan McNamara
Nathan Weida
Nichola Smalley
Nicholas Brown
Nicholas Rutherford
Nick Chapman
Nick James
Nick Marshall
Nick Nelson & Rachel
  Eley

Nick Sidwell
Nick Twemlow
Nicola Hart
Nicola Mira
Nicolas Sampson
Nicole Matteini
Nicoletta Asciuto
Niki Sammut
Nina Todorova
Niven Kumar
Noah Brumfield
Norma Gillespie
Norman Batchelor
Odilia Corneth
Olga Zilberbourg
Owen Williams
Paavan Buddhdev
Pamela Ritchie
Pankaj Mishra
Pat Winslow
Patricia Beesley
Patricia Gurton
Patrick Hoare
Patrick King
Patrick McGuinness
Paul Bangert
Paul Cray
Paul Ewing
Paul Gibson
Paul Jones
Paul Munday
Paul Myatt
Paul Nightingale
Paul Scott
Paul Segal
Paula Melendez
Pavlos Stavropoulos
Pawel Szeliga
Penelope Hewett Brown
Penelope Hewett-Brown
Perlita Payne
Peter Griffin
Peter Hayden
Peter Rowland
Peter Wells
Peter and Nancy Ffitch
Petra Hendrickson

Petra Stapp
Philip Herbert
Philip Leichauer
Philip Warren
Phillipa Clements
Phoebe Millerwhite
Piet Van Bockstal
Prakash Nayak
Priya Sharma
Rachael de Moravia
Rachael Williams
Rachel Beddow
Rachel Belt
Rachel Carter
Rachel Gaughan
Rachel Van Riel
Rahul Kanakia
Rajni Aldridge
Ralph Jacobowitz
Ramona Pulsford
Ramya Purkanti
Rebecca Caldwell
Rebecca Carter
Rebecca Maddox
Rebecca Marriott
Rebecca Michel
Rebecca Moss
Rebecca Parry
Rebecca Rushforth
Rebecca Shaak
Rebecca Surin
Renee Thomas
Rhea Pokorny
Rhiannon Armstrong
Rich Sutherland
Richard Dew
Richard Ellis
Richard Gwyn
Richard Harrison
Richard Mansell
Richard Shea
Richard Soundy
Richard Village
Rita Kaar
Rita Marrinson
Rita O'Brien
Robbie Matlock

Robert Gillett
Robert Hamilton
Robert Wolff
Roberto Hull
Robin McLean
Robin Taylor
Roger Ramsden
Ronan O'Shea
Rory Williamson
Rosabella Reeves
Rosalind May
Rosalind Ramsay
Rosanna Foster
Rosemary Horsewood
Rosie Sparrowhawk
Royston Tester
Royston Tester
Roz Simpson
Rupert Ziziros
Ruth Curry
Ryan Day
Ryan Oliver
Ryan Pierce
Sally Ayhan
Sally Baker
Sally Warner
Sally Warner
Sam Gordon
Samuel Crosby
Sara Bea
Sara Kittleson
Sara Unwin
Sarah Arboleda
Sarah Brewer
Sarah Lucas
Sarah Manvel
Sarah Stevns
Satyam Makoieva
Scott Chiddister
Sean Johnston
Sean Kottke
Sean McGivern
Selina Guinness
Severijn Hagemeijer
Shannon Knapp
Sharon Dilworth
Sharon McCammon

Sharon Rhodes
Shaun Whiteside
Sian Hannah
Sienna Kang
Silje Bergum Kinsten
Simak Ali
Simon Pitney
Simon Robertson
Simone Martelossi
SK Grout
Sophie Nappert
Sophie Rees
Stacy Rodgers
Stefano Mula
Stephan Eggum
Stephanie Miller
Stephanie Wasek
Stephen Eisenhammer
Stephen Fuller
Stephen Pearsall
Stephen Yates
Steve Chapman
Steve Clough
Steve Dearden
Steve Tuffnell
Steven Hess
Steven Norton
Stewart Eastham
Stuart Allen
Stuart Grey
Stuart Wilkinson
Sujani Reddy
Susan Edsall
Susan Ferguson
Susan Jaken
Susan Wachowski
Susan Winter
Suzanne and Nick Davies
Suzanne Kirkham
Sylvie Zannier-Betts
Tania Hershman
Tara Roman
Tatjana Soli
Tatyana Reshetnik
Taylor Ffitch
Teresa Werner
Tess Lewis

Tess Lewis
Tessa Lang
The Mighty Douche
  Softball Team
Theo Voortman
Therese Oulton
Thom Keep
Thomas Alt
Thomas Campbell
Thomas Fritz
Thomas Noone
Thomas van den Bout
Tiffany Lehr
Tim Kelly
Tina Rotherham-
  Winqvist
Tina Juul Møller

Toby Ryan
Tom Darby
Tom Doyle
Tom Franklin
Tom Gray
Tom McAllister
Tom Stafford
Tom Whatmore
Tracy Bauld
Tracy Lee-Newman
Tracy Northup
Trevor Latimer
Trevor Wald
Turner Docherty
Val Challen
Valerie O'Riordan
Vanessa Dodd

Vanessa Heggie
Vanessa Nolan
Vanessa Rush
Veronica Barnsley
Victor Meadowcroft
Victor Saouma
Victoria Goodbody
Victoria Huggins
Vijay Pattisapu
Wendy Langridge
William Brockenborough
William Orton
William Schwaber
William Schwartz
William Wilson
Zachary Maricondia
Zoe Thomas